PRAISE F

In *Bliss*, Fredrick Soukup has put together a story of loss and longing in simple language that drags the reader into the story, wrapping them in want and worry. His characters are rich and deep and inescapable.

– William Alton, author of *The Tragedy of Being Happy*

Bliss is deft, moving, and sharply observed, seamlessly weaving together the affluent, superficial world of the suburbs with that of an inner city neighborhood pulsing with energy and danger. But if Frederick Soukup's novel is a skillful evocation of time and place, it also tells the timeless story of a young man on a quest to find out where—and with whom—he belongs.

– Laurie Ann Doyle, author of *World Gone Missing*, winner of the Alligator Juniper National Fiction Award, and the 2018 Nautilus Award Winner

BLISS

Fredrick Soukup

Regal House Publishing

Published by
Regal House Publishing, LLC
Raleigh, NC 27612

ISBN -13 (paperback): 9781947548992
ISBN -13 (epub): 9781646030262
Library of Congress Control Number: 2019941542

Interior and cover design by Lafayette & Greene
lafayetteandgreene.com
Cover images © by Oleg Podzorov/Shutterstock

Regal House Publishing, LLC
https://regalhousepublishing.com

Printed in the United States of America

To Mom and Dad

PART ONE

Five grand in savings intended for his first semester at the University of Minnesota Medical School affords Connor first and last months' rent, two months of job searching, and several cases of beer. Sleepless summer in South Chicago. Teens fight in the streets. At night police sirens whine like starving infants. In the afternoon he perches on the landing of the staircase zigzagging down the side of his apartment complex, watching the bus stop below exchange the city's elderly and hobbled and stoned, its airport workers and gas station clerks and toddlers clutching their mothers' hands for balance. Craterous potholes dictate the monotonous swerves of traffic. On the other side of the street, shattered windows honeycomb the burnt-orange brick building identical to his; on the moonlit sidewalk, glass like shards of gold glints, which curfew-less schoolkids gleefully chuck at streetlights.

He sleeps late, watches movies on his computer, orders-in Chinese and deep dish. He gets drunk night after night and gains belly chub. Thankful whenever the unreliable internet connection abbreviates his job hunt, he closes his laptop and naps, somehow exhausted. His father, Bill, calls him once a day, every day. Occasionally, Connor answers.

"You short on money?"

"I'll have a job soon."

"Where?"

"I'm going to bed."

"It's only seven."

"I have to work on an application first."

"Finance is a good career, Connor. We could get you licensed, you know. You could work with me, or at another office if you don't want to see me too much. At least till you figure something else out."

"Thanks. I'll think about it."

"Or, you could lie to me and say you're taking night classes, or blogging, or training to be a cage fighter. Something."

"I'm trying out for a reality TV show."

"That's more like it. Say, I could get you set up at a branch there. Even part-time, you could make some money."

"I should go. Love you."

"Love you, too. Give me your address, Connor."

"A check might not make it to me, anyway."

"Still could try. How long will you be gone?"

"I don't know."

Connor's neighbor, Lee, eats Connor's food, drinks Connor's beer, and pawns Connor's clothes for junk money. Connor misses him when he's gone. One evening Lee says he's leaving town to see his sister in Charlotte.

"Thought you said she lived in Durham?"

"What's the difference to *you*?"

The beer bottles in his backpack clink together as Lee rushes out of the apartment.

At four in the morning, he knocks on Connor's door. Connor opens it to find him sweating and shivering under a yellowing bedsheet, the corner of which he's balled up and stuffed in his mouth to staunch the bleeding from a lost front tooth.

Lee meanders in, sits cross-legged on the splintered kitchen linoleum.

"The fuck happened?"

"Don't know," Lee mumbles into the cloth clot. "You got any beer?"

"You don't know what happened to your tooth?"

"And I don't miss it, either."

Connor pours a glass of water, asks to look inside Lee's mouth.

Lee opens wide.

"Could get infected," Connor says.

"You a doctor?"

"No. Pre-med, though."

"Fuck that."

"You should go to the hospital."

"I'll sleep it off. Just got carried away."

"Let's go," Connor says, holding out his hand. "I'll call an Uber."

"No one's getting us."

"We'll walk, then."

"I got an immune system like a dumpster, fuck you mean."

"Did you overdose?"

"You'll know it when you see it."

"I don't want to see that."

"Get high with me, you won't notice a thing," Lee quips.

"Right."

"Stop stressing out. Everything's cool."

Lee stands, stick-thin and hunched, the black mustache above his lip crusted darkly with blood. He's thirty-six, though the fleshy bags under his eyes belong to a man twenty years older. He tightens the sheet around his shoulders and smirks at Connor, who hands him the glass of water. He drinks it in two gulps.

"I got a wife. Got two boys across town and a good gig working construction when they take me back. Even got a degree in astronomics, fuck you mean. Bring me some beers over, would you," he says, as he shuffles out of the apartment, slamming the door behind him.

At the library, two bus transfers away, Connor reads magazines and newspapers and blogposts, eyeing vagrants who exploit the lax bathroom policy by washing up with wet, soapy paper towels and, as winter approaches, by shooting up in the stalls. They call him Fruity, because, instead of money, he gives them apples and oranges. They tell him about their murdered brothers and imprisoned aunts, about their wealthy cousins who moved away and don't call anymore. They tell him Lee's wife left him when one of their boys drowned in an inflatable backyard swimming pool many summers ago.

He switches to vodka mixed into half full lemonade containers, whiskey into pop bottles, and drinks while he walks the city, thinking about how much money he has left, how he'd fare in a fight with the tougher strangers he passes, about writing poetry and learning to play an instrument. About farming a plot of land, his future wife and children. About why religion has prevailed so long on this planet, why music is beautiful, why ketchup tastes so much better than mustard. About sex.

"What are you reading right now?" Bill asks.

"The newspaper. There are always copies at the library."

"A day late?"

"Free."

"I'll pay for a subscription," Bill offers. "They'll take them right to your place."

"It's better this way. Things are okay, Dad. You're worrying too much."

"That's what I'm supposed to do."

"Jesus Christ."

"What?"

"Okay, then. It's nothing. It's good. Thank you."

On the first snowfall of the season, four scrawny preteens fan out on the sidewalk so he can't pass. He steps out onto the dead street and they circle him. He tries to play it cool, tells them he has no money, then raises his fists and turns in a circle as they lunge toward and away from him, taunting. He cowers. They rap him on the skull a few times, and since he left his wallet between his mattress and bedsprings, they take his booze and jacket. He runs home, sits on the floor of the scum-slick shower, head down, arms on his knees, catching water in his palms. Then he clenches his fists.

He stays in bed for two days, until Lee cheers him up with a bowl of cold off-brand cereal. The spoiled milk makes him ill. He loses ten pounds vomiting. He goes off the grid. No library, internet, blogs, emails, calls, or texts. He does push-ups and sit-ups and leans his mattress up against his bedroom wall as a punching bag. He considers buying a handgun.

"That's stupid," Lee says, smoking a spliff by Connor's cracked bedroom window. "Stupid as fuck."

"What about mace?"

"Or a rape whistle?" Lee says. He takes a hit. "I know what you should do."

"You got all the answers."

"You're overthinking everything. It's sad as hell."

"Fuck you."

"If you plan on being an idiot, you might as well go all the way. Stick around, knock up some women. Get hooked on junk, like me. Meanwhile, buy a gun and blast those kids away."

"None of that will happen."

"I know. Because you're going back to Minneapolis."

"There's nothing there for me."

"Nothing here, either, you selfish little fucker. Stupid, stupid, stupid…" Lee shakes his head as he hands Connor the spliff and leaves the apartment.

Two days later, just after midnight, Connor notices Lee's door cracked. He steps inside and finds him quivering in bed. Sweat dewdrops tremble on his forehead. The drenched bedsheets reek of body odor and vomit. One by one Lee has plucked out mustache hairs with his fingers; dozens of whiskers pepper his pillowcase.

Connor squats next to the bed, takes Lee's wrist, and begins to measure his pulse.

"Fuck are you doing?"

"Stay still."

"Don't pull that shit."

"I'm calling an ambulance. I'll be right back. Hang tight."

Lee grabs Connor's arm. "You don't know nothing. Don't call nobody. Don't pull that shit. I'm not making a scene."

"We'll meet them out front. You could die."

"This is nothing. I'm going to sleep. Get the fuck out of my apartment."

"Carol can drive us in."

"Carol don't pull shit, fuck you mean."

"What would your sons do if they were me?"

Lee bares his teeth at him, showing off the gap in his top row, then bites his bottom lip. He rolls onto his back and looks at the ceiling. "I have my PhD in Ultra-Physicism, you cocky prick. Go get Carol."

Connor jogs to the building across the street. Lee's friend Carol doesn't answer the door. When he returns, Lee's door is locked.

Connor applies for an auto parts warehouse gig six blocks away. The hiring manager happens to be the former father-in-law of one of the library junkies, who offers to put in a good word for him.

"I don't know, man," Connor says. "Was it an ugly divorce?"

"You know a pretty one? Wouldn't do it if it wouldn't help," the man replies, peeling an orange with his cruddy fingernails. His bone-white hair is parted in the middle, ponytailed in the back with a rubber band. Last month he lost his glasses. Now he squints.

"How come *you* don't work for him?"

"I'm self-employed. And last I saw my wife, she woke me up with a hot curling iron on my ass-cheek."

"Whatever you think, I guess."

Awaiting the warehouse's decision, he watches every Academy Award-nominated film of the past forty years and texts with Vanessa, an ex-girlfriend from college. She works nights at a movie theater to help pay the U of M's Master of Social Work program tuition. She says she admires him for doing his own thing, though she offers to hook him up with a ticket-tearer post at the theater, should he come home. Soon they're sexting.

He jogs five miles a day, loses his paunch, and gains three pounds of muscle. His knuckles crack and bleed from the cold night air. His tawny beard is thin on his cheeks, but thick around his mouth and below his chin. His chestnut hair is long beneath his stocking cap. His eyes sink beneath his greasy tallow complexion, glimmers of guttering candlelight.

"You changed your profile picture on Facebook," Bill says. "You're looking thin."

"Been running every day."

"Hair's getting long. And the beard."

"Sure."

"You going to church there?" Bill asks.

Connor drops his head, pinches his eyes shut, and taps his phone against his forehead.

"You hear stories about kids is all," Bill says. "Sometimes, people just slip into…different ways of thinking. Like, you're off the grid. Maybe you're getting into trouble, or under some type of spell…"

"It's not religion, Dad. Just a beard. I can't afford razors, and I have nothing and no one to shave for. It doesn't look that bad, and anyway there's nothing wrong with Islam."

"Of course not. I just…you're spending so much time alone, reading books. I guess…well, nobody knows…fathers worry. What do you do with all your time there?" Bill asks.

"I run, look for work. I get tired and go to sleep. I don't even have the energy to face Mecca these days."

"Don't have to be a jerk about it," Bill says.

"Could've played along and duped you if I wanted to."

"By the way, you have to start on your student loans, unless you want to join the army or something."

"I got it."

"Really?"

"I got it."

"Connor, did med school really reject you?"

Connor scratches his beard with his phone.

Bill continues, "One of your professors called my office. She couldn't believe it."

"Fuck, Dad."

"Just tell the truth."

"I wish I'd gotten rejected."

They're silent for half a minute, then Bill asks once more if Connor needs money.

The next morning the warehouse calls to tell him he cleared his background check, and he accepts a graveyard shift cleaning the facility and prepping the next day's shipments. He celebrates with a beer downtown, then buys a used bike for his commute. On his second shift he leaves it outside, leaning against the back entrance; in the morning, it's missing. To punish himself for his carelessness, he starts walking to work.

The dusty florescent lightbulbs streaking across the ceiling have begun to blacken, lending the building the ambience of a morgue. Ceiling-high racks line the walls, cluttered with hoods and bumpers and fenders and doors, some unpackaged and glossy, some bound in foam and cellophane or boxed up. He makes a pot of coffee and plays music on the office stereo. Then he vacuums and wipes down the upstairs managerial offices and employee lounge. Afterward, he descends the metal staircase to the concrete floor, where for the rest of the night he readies the following day's orders. Prepping only takes two hours, so he sweeps and mops, sets traps for the mice nesting among stale inventory long ago rotated into the darker corners of the warehouse. A decaying raccoon carcass, which he scoops out with a plastic shovel and tosses into the dumpster out back, makes him gag. For the final hours of his shifts, just before dawn, he eats breakfast and reads the newspaper, calculating his budget in the margins of the sports section or underlining for his memory the names of prominent bank executives, politicians, and lawyers. He thinks about Vanessa.

Interested in everything but medicine, he checks out library books about international trade agreements and sanctions, beads bartered amid Sudanese conflict, the World Wars, existentialism, OPEC, the IMF, Bohemian anti-Jewish pogroms, Bolshevism, and Industrial Revolution working conditions. His hair and beard lengthen. His chest broadens. He spends part of his first check on work boots and fresh vegetables at a market fifteen minutes away by bus. He attends Narcotics Anonymous meetings in a nearby church basement, and on his day off, weather permitting, plays chess in a small treeless park with one of the members, an old woman who wears ankle-length corduroy dresses. When she finally asks him about his drug problem and he admits he's never had one, she collects her chess pieces and board and leaves. At their next meeting, no one looks him in the eye. He doesn't attend another.

He begins running two miles a day. Three. Five. Extension-cord spindly. He earns a ten-cent-an-hour raise and picks up an evening job bartending. He argues politics and religion with the regulars, helps them back onto their stools when they fall off.

One night at the warehouse, while shoveling the back entrance sidewalk, he spots his bike sticking out of a shallow frozen pond. He breaks up the ice and pulls the bike free.

The next day he buys a lock.

Vanessa says she wants to visit him in Chicago some weekend.

"You'd come here?"

"You don't want me to?"

"It's not great."

"And?"

"I mean, I want to see you," he says.

"And you're not coming home now, so…"

"Not much to do here."

"I'll drive."

"Take the bus. Your car might get jacked."

"It's not that nice of a car."

"You'll see. I'm sorry. Take the bus."

He scrubs the shower, cleans the fridge. He meets her downtown and they ride the bus back to his apartment. Her things are packed in a large purse. She's gangly, with copper eyes, wavy honey blonde hair that reaches her shoulders, and a white scar running vertically from the corner of her mouth. Her complexion is creamy, lightly rouged. He puts his arm around her. She squeezes his thigh. "Saw your dad at the theater. He told me to bring you back with me."

"He'd like that."

"He said you don't want him to visit."

"That's not true."

"He was with a woman."

"No, he wasn't."

"Whoever it was, it wasn't their first date."

"Sneaky."

"When I moved out, my parents got a dog."

Back at his apartment, he hangs her coat over the front door handle and puts her purse in his bedroom. She asks if she can take a shower. He leads her down the hallway to the bathroom, shows her where the towels are and how to deal with the tricky faucet. The bathroom is so small that she has to step into the tub to open the door fully. She pulls him close to shut the door behind him, then he steps back against it. She runs shower water. As she tells him about the professors and students she's met in orientation, all the officious and dull and charming and kind people, she undresses to her black bra and panties, neatly folds her sweatshirt and shirt and jeans and socks, and stacks them on the sink. The mirror fogs. She fingers a condom from her jeans pocket and places it atop her clothes.

After showering, they sit in the living room, drinking whiskey from coffee mugs and eating Chinese food from paper boxes. She tucks her hair into the back of her hoodie.

"You're hiding," she says.

"No."

"You are. You'd probably enjoy med school. You'd do well. I know you would."

"Tell me more about your program," he replies.

"See. You don't want to talk about you."

They switch boxes.

"Are you depressed?" she asks.

"I was before."

"I've never slept with someone with so much facial hair."

"I'm honored."

She giggles, a few quiet huffs. "I didn't know I liked whiskey," she says.

"It's nothing much."

"If you're not hiding, I don't know what you're up to, Connor."

"You say my name funny."

"Because I like you."

"It *is* a long bus ride," he replies.

She giggles again, finishes her mug, and stands. Stretching her arms above her head, she draws a deep breath and inspects the ceiling and walls. "Maybe you're just special," she says.

He closes the lids on the boxes and puts the leftovers in the fridge. When he comes back, she's holding his mug and smirking. In her eyes are hints of lime. "What is it?" he asks.

"Nothing."

"What?"

"Let me cut your hair."

He shakes his head.

"Just a trim," she pleads.

"I know what you're trying to do."

"What's that?"

"You know, too," he says. "What would you cut it with, anyway?" She grins at him as she goes to his bedroom for her purse, then returns with scissors. "I know what you're trying to do."

"You have no idea, Connor."

He carries his office chair into the living room, takes his shirt off, and sits. She removes her hoodie, beneath which she wears a tight black shirt. She straddles him. Resting her elbows on his shoulders, clutching his hair with one hand and the scissors with the other, she kisses his lips and cheeks and neck. Her exhalations, the scent of hot liquor, pleases his skin. He unbuttons his jeans, but she whispers, "Wait." Then she leans away and tells him not to move. As she snips at his beard, loose hairs tickle his bare chest and she pauses to blow them off.

He murmurs so to keep his face still. "What did the woman look like, the one with my dad?"

"Blonde, younger than he is. Sexy."

"Sexier than you?"

"Might be. Does he date much?"

"Never."

"Probably misses you."

"Your parents should point him to an animal shelter."

"You're funny when you're homeless."

"I'm not homeless."

"Just about."

"Not even close. Anyway, I like it here."

She brushes hair from his shoulder, cocks her head back to assess the symmetry of her efforts, her eyes shifting slightly from side to side. "My program is full of lost souls who don't know they're lost," she says, trimming again. "Nice boys and girls with no fucking clue."

"Not you, though. You got it all figured out."

"I'm not the one laying low, shoveling up rodent carcasses, eating hotdogs every night."

"That was only for a week; I was too lazy to go to the grocery store. For the record, I doubt I can ever stomach another hotdog."

"At least you're admitting that you're lost."

"I guess."

"We're all just kind of pushed along from high schools to colleges to hospitals or law firms or government positions or shitty desk jobs. We rack up debt, then get unfulfilling jobs that we don't like so we can pay it off. And a lot of what we do is based on the illusion that we're doing something meaningful for others, but most of the time it's only for ourselves."

"You always were a bit of a downer when you drank."

"Just being honest. Sit still." She lifts his chin with her finger, snips at his neck hairs. "Because if we're lucky enough to get pushed along like we are, then we have no idea what it's like for those who aren't so lucky, the ones we're told we're helping. And how can we help them if we don't understand what they've been through? *Really* help? Like I said, we're lost souls."

"You're even more cynical than I am. Can I ask why, if it's all a sham anyway, you don't just go the smash-and-grab business route like a bunch in our class did?"

"Because maybe I won't always be so lucky. Maybe down the road I'll understand misfortune better than I do now. In the meantime, I won't delude myself into thinking I'm changing the world merely because I chose to be a social worker instead of a consultant, and because of this, maybe at some point I'll actually be able to do some good for others in need, even if by accident."

"Fair enough."

"Why did you come here?"

"You have better reasons for continuing school than I have for not."

"I'd still like to hear them."

"Tell me more about this woman my dad was with."

"You go first."

"Were they serious? Like, were they holding hands?"

"It's your turn," she pressed him.

"I was sad."

"But you're not anymore."

"I'm not anymore," he echoes her.

"So go back, explain to the U of M what happened, and start classes next semester."

"If I go back, I'll feel the way I felt before I got here. My mom was sad, too, before she split on us one day. I don't know why she left; I was little then. But I bet I was having the same feelings she had, and I can't imagine letting them fester till it's not just my dad I'm abandoning."

"Let *what* fester?"

"I felt numb, like nothing mattered. Like everyone was comatose except for me, but I'd be out, too, soon enough, just like them."

"You feel better now?"

"Chicago's been good to me…I just need to experience something else for a while."

She looks him over, nibbling on her bottom lip. "Well, I

only saw your dad and her briefly. It seemed like they really like each other."

"Always told him to date, but he wouldn't."

"He must really miss you."

"I'll come back soon enough."

She leans away to inspect his beard again, clips a few more strands, and drops the scissors to her bellybutton. When she takes off her shirt and uses it to wipe the hairs from his collar and chest, he pulls her close. She drops the scissors and hugs him, cradling his head in her arms, rubbing her cheek against him.

"Remind me, what happened to your lip. The scar," he says.

"Neighbor's dog bit me when I was a girl."

"How does my beard look?"

"I didn't take much off, but it looks cleaner."

"Can't believe you came all this way."

"You'll return the favor sometime," she replies as she climbs off him. "You just have to suck it up, be an adult like the rest of us are trying to."

They drink more whiskey, talk until morning, then sleep all day.

She goes to the warehouse with him the following night, cruises the internet on her phone while he works. The next day they nap and make love and order pizza and drink all his beer. He promises to visit her in Minnesota soon.

That evening, on the bus ride to the station, they're quiet. Sleet splatters against the window. She holds his hand in her lap, from time to time lifting it to her lips and kissing it wetly.

The following morning, he calls home. "Anything new, Dad?"

"Not really. You haven't been answering your phone."

"Been busy."

Bill says, "I thought you might've met somebody...or that you had a visitor..."

"It does get lonely. Sometimes it's nice to get out of the house, catch a movie..."

"She told me she went to see you."

"And she told me she saw you at the theater," Connor replies.

"It's not what you think, though."

"I don't care, Dad. You should do what you want. It's *good* that you're seeing someone."

To fill the uncomfortable silence, Bill makes a *clicking* noise into the phone. Then he splutters, "Okay. Okay, then. Thank you. But when are you coming home? Vanessa's lovely as ever. Charlotte and I had her over for dinner recently. You'll like Charlotte. She's lovely, too. Everyone's lovely. I want you to meet her. If you're here, you might as well. So you'll come back in the spring. And for good. Great. I'm glad that's settled."

"We'll see."

"So glad Vanessa went to see you. She's the best. Really, even if you don't want to come home and see me, you have to come and see her."

"Dad."

That night Connor steps out of the market, onto the blustery street, holding a bag of groceries. He asks the two men standing out front if they saw anyone take his bike, which he left unlocked on the sidewalk. They snicker and shake their heads no.

"How come they didn't take that one?" he asks, pointing at one leaning against the brick façade of the market, a band of red tape on its handlebars. The men erupt in laughter and he walks home with his pasta, sauce, and milk.

For two weeks, each evening before he goes to work and Vanessa goes to bed, they talk on the phone, making plans for future visits, for his potential return. For two weeks, he works and sleeps and drinks and schemes.

One morning after work, he can't sleep. He throws on sweatpants and a thrift store jacket, takes two shots of whiskey, and starts walking back toward the warehouse. He turns on the side street that takes him past a recreation center, where he spots a hunk of black steel on the concrete steps of the entrance. He walks closer to examine the bike, and recognizing the scratches on the frame, he goes inside. The building smells of sweaty feet and tangy plastic. He walks toward the sounds of shouts and squeaky shoes in the gym.

"You need something?" asks a young woman at the reception desk behind him. He turns to face her and she leans over the desk, her eyebrows raised, her olive-green eyes fierce and eager. It seems to him she's hoping he'll say something stupid or rude, so she can set him straight. He looks down at the carpet as he walks toward her, then absently drums his fingertips on the desk.

"Somebody stole my bike," he says, pretending to read a laminated flyer taped to the desk. "It's out front."

"You sure?"

He stops drumming, looks up. She hasn't leaned back or lowered her eyebrows. A thin white headband gathers the black curls at the back of her head. She wears jeans and a men's long-sleeved knitted undershirt cut two inches down the front.

"Absolutely," he says.

"You acted like you were going to try something in here."

Embarrassed, he shakes his head, smiling coyly. He glances down at the flyer, runs his fingertips over its edges. "I'm sorry," he says. "Didn't mean to worry you."

"I'm not worried about me." She steps back and slouches into the swivel chair behind her. She pushes her sleeves to her elbows and crosses her arms, exposing the black calligraphic tattoos on her wrists and thin forearms. Then she cocks her head to the side and smiles at him. "Fucked up this morning, huh?" she asks, amused.

"Just a drink to help me sleep."

"Up all night?"

"Just got off of work."

"Right. Those are my nephews is all."

"All of them?"

"Yep."

"They sound too old to be your nephews."

"Most of them are kids," she replies.

"I don't know what I was going to do. I mean, I wasn't going to do anything. I just want my bike back."

"Go on, then."

"I had momentum before you stopped me. Now I'm too nervous."

"Just kids."

"*Your* nephews, though."

"You want me to go in with you?" she heckles him.

She stares at him, and for a few seconds, before looking down at the flyer again, he stares back. "Guess I could just take it back," he says. "Maybe I'll do that."

"Where you from?"

"Around here."

"No, you're not."

"Minneapolis, originally."

"You a junkie?" she asks.

"Just skinny."

"I have an aunt in Minneapolis. So, you came here to *what*, bike?"

It's been so long since he last laughed, his cheek muscles hurt. She locks her hands above her head and stretches her arms as she spins once in the chair. Her small, smooth hands turn. Facing him again, she stops the chair and stands. Then she leads him down the hallway to the gym. The high bay lights above are grimy; the room is dim. The sheen of the plastic tiles has worn off. Some guys, teenage to early twenties, are playing full-court five-on-five. Three sit on the lone row of bleachers on the side, texting or listening to music on their phones. Each player, shirtless, wearing baggy shorts or sweatpants, is either eight-pack skinny or obese.

"Timeout," she yells. The guy at the top of the key stops dribbling and holds the ball at his hip, and they turn to face Connor and the woman. "Demetrius!" she yells to the shortest, thinnest boy in the gym, standing at the three-point line on the other side of the court.

"I didn't do nothing!" the kid shouts back.

"Don't steal this man's bike."

"I didn't do it."

"Demetrius."

"Yes, ma'am," he mumbles.

"What did you say?" she shouts.

"I won't do it again, I said!"

"Thank you, Demetrius," she replies sweetly.

As she leads Connor out of the gym, he looks back at them. They break into laughter as soon as he's out of sight. He can't tell if they're laughing at him or the boy.

On the way outside, she grabs a roll of red tape from the desk.

"You must have ten sisters," he says. "How much is a membership?"

"Five hundred."

"That's a lot."

She looks up at him. "You can pay in installments if you need to."

"Can't tell if you're joking," he says.

"Can't tell if you're gullible."

She opens the front door for him and they walk out into

the squally winter afternoon. Cigarette butts, pop cans, and crumbled receipts speckle the cracked concrete front steps. She lights a cigarette, then, using her teeth, tears off a strip of tape, which she wraps around the frame.

"Maybe you should tell him not to steal *any* bikes."

"It's not just for him."

"How did you know it was him, then?"

She rolls her eyes at him.

"What's your name?" he asks.

"It's not like that," she says, flashing her eyes at him as she stands.

"Not like what?"

"Run along, white boy."

She smiles and breathes deeply through her nose. He stands his bike, walks it away from the rec center. When he looks back, her eyes are closed.

Back at his apartment, he eats a bowl of cereal while reading the day-old newspaper, then he searches for his razor and the scissors Vanessa left him. In the bathroom mirror, he sees how sallow his flesh has become over the past months. Though, against his pale complexion his turquoise eyes luster starkly.

He fingers a tuft of bangs and begins to cut.

❧

No blood, no foul.

Every morning after work, Connor changes into black shorts and a gray shirt in the rec center locker room and plays basketball with the guys for an hour. Every morning, he goes home scored with fresh slap marks and scratches on his arms, neck, and back. The day he finally asks them what her name is, they tell him it's Danielle, then hack him especially hard throughout the next game. That morning he eats eggs and toast at his kitchen table, clean-shaven, hair buzzed short, shirtless, stinging all over. Holding a bag of frozen corn to the swelling black eye he got from a loose elbow, disregarding the many notifications on his phone, the texts and calls from Bill and Vanessa, he smiles.

"They crucified you again," Danielle tells him as he walks by her desk. Sitting in her swivel chair, she wears jeans, an oversized wool sweater, and orchid lipstick. "Just wait till it warms up and you play out on the gravel."

"They'll lighten up by then."

"Not if you keep driving to the basket."

"That's my game."

"I've seen you play; you don't have any game," she says. "You drinking this morning?"

"That was a one-off type of thing."

"You cleaned up."

"You like it?" he asks.

"You look less like a perpetrator."

"That's nice of you to say. Is this place hiring?"

She ignores him.

"Really, are you?"

"Just volunteers for afterschool programs."

"Can I get an application?"

She stares at him, slack-jawed, tongue in her cheek, then opens a desk drawer. She hands him the application but doesn't let go when he grabs it. "Don't do this for stupid reasons."

"Like what?"

"A lot of the kids here don't get much attention at home, so they get attached to people real quick. If they start trusting you, they're *very* trusting. They need tons of consistency and patience. You understand?"

He nods.

"You do?"

He nods again.

"If I find out you're not doing this one hundred percent for them, the authorities will never find your body. Okay?"

"Okay."

She pinches the paper between her slender fingers. They stare at each other.

"Okay," he repeats.

She lets go.

He quits the bar and signs up for two four-hour shifts each week at the center. He tries to follow her example, observing as she skillfully mediates the kids' quarrels, amuses them with goofy dance moves and playful pranks at his expense. At first she and the three other volunteers put him in charge of managing two-dozen inhalers during dodgeball, but the kids take to him and he graduates to kickball pitcher and umpire. He hands out snacks, breaks up fights, and helps with homework.

What he gleans from the kids disturbs his dreams, leads him trance-like through his overnight warehouse shifts. Boys whose foster mothers beat them with metal coat hangers. Probation officers trading good reports for sex. Girls drugged up by the men they love, turning fifty tricks a night. Incarcerated breadwinners. Toddlers molested by their parents. The undocumented and uninsured and unemployed. Cancer and booze and heart disease and tumors and bullet wounds and obesity and depression and pills and schizophrenia. Refugees from Somalia and Iraq and Sudan and Yemen. Cops frisking parents in the center hallway in front of their children.

All the families trying.

He meets her shy, smiley, handsome, actual nephews, EJ and Marquees. EJ is in second grade. Not quite old enough for school, Marquees spends his days with his mom or at the center playing basketball. After school, EJ and Marquees chase each other in the hallway, hang out with the other kids, and nap in the office behind Danielle.

When the center is slow, Connor sometimes rebounds for them as they squat and leap like frogs to thrust the ball toward the hoop, or plays cards with them, all three sitting cross-legged on the gym floor. Mimicking the center regulars, they call him Milky, though not in front of their aunt.

One afternoon, while Danielle smokes out front, Marquees trips and burns his knee on the hallway carpet. Crying, he throws his hands up at Connor, who picks him up and fans his hand over the wound until the boy hushes.

Later, playing cards, they talk about how their uncle works on cars, how whenever they see him he stinks of oil.

"Only on the weekends, though," EJ says.

"He only smells like that on the weekends?" Connor asks.

"No, we only see him then."

"You go to your aunt's during the week, though?"

"Sometimes."

Whenever she has a moment, Danielle is busy on the front desk computer. "I thought maybe you were messing around on Facebook, but now I'm not so sure," Connor says to her on his way out one day. "Can I ask what you're working on?"

"No," she replies, eyes on the screen.

He pauses, wanting to have something more to say, then he jogs out the door.

After Vanessa completes the first semester of her program, she and Connor each drink a celebratory bottle of white wine during a three-hour Skype chat on his night off. During their second pours—hers into a voluminous wineglass, his into a metal cup the previous tenants left behind—the glee in his voice while describing the center betrays him.

He's never heard her tone so curt. "I thought you planned on coming home soon."

"I did."

"When? Minnesota has warehouses, too, FYI."

"I'm not here because of the warehouse."

"I know. You're doing your self-discovery shit. Let me know when you grow out of it."

"What if I don't?"

"Well..." She pauses, then purses her lips as if her wine has soured. "Are you saying you might not?"

"I'm just trying to challenge myself."

"My hero," she replies, pressing her hands against her heart.

"It's not for you. I'm doing it for myself."

"You're playing basketball and moving car parts and eating macaroni for dinner every night. Quit being so dramatic."

Now they drink straight from their bottles. For half an hour, he brags about his self-sufficiency, his credit rating and relatively minimal debt, intermittently listing his various wholesome meals. Meanwhile, she chastises him for being "an adrenaline-junkie," "a pathetic voyeur," and "a coward." But by the time they slosh down the last of their wine, its tartness lost on drunk tongues, they forget how their fight began and he vows to come north for a visit soon. Making up is a competition to see who can promise more. She promises to be patient with him; he promises to take her out dancing. She promises to give him space; he promises to have a sit-down dinner at her parents' house and explain to them his future plans, which, he assures her, he'll solidify before then. Before ending the call, she kisses the camera on her computer.

The next afternoon his phone buzzes. Hungover in bed, he impulsively answers the call, then immediately curses.

"Vanessa says you're coming to visit!"

"Please don't holler, Dad. I have a headache."

"I'm buying you a plane ticket right now. I can cover you if you miss work, too."

"I haven't made any plans yet."

"Why did you tell her you would?"

"Why did *she* tell you I would?"

"She texted me this morning. She said you promised her last night. This is getting ridiculous. Just come for a few days."

Connor drops the phone into the folds of his blanket and rubs his temples with his middle fingers. As if aware that Connor has tuned him out, Bill raises his voice, and the muffled, strained chirping of his complaints so harasses Connor that he picks up the phone and cuts his father off mid-sentence. "I'll take the bus."

"That's stupid. I'm buying a plane ticket. If it makes you feel better, you can keep a tab and pay me back later. No, don't waste time on the bus—there's so much I have to tell you."

"Can't you just tell me over the phone?"

"No, I can't."

Connor pauses and replies, "Okay, okay. Fine. I'm being selfish. I'm sorry."

"You sound like hell, by the way. It'll be good for you to get out for a bit. How's May?"

"June's better."

"That works. Thank you, thank you, thank you. I'm so happy!" Exhilarated, Bill begins to shout, tacking nails into the sides of Connor's head. As instinctively as he answered, Connor hangs up.

As his departure date approaches, each conversation with Vanessa is more pleasant than the last. His dad stops pestering him about his health and finances, careful not to inadvertently change his son's mind. Connor texts college friends about getting together for a drink and browses Bill's Facebook page for pictures of Charlotte. Unfortunately, however, Bill hasn't updated his page since he signed up five years ago.

Throughout the final hour of his shifts, while Connor fights the urge to drink the cup of coffee that will make it too hard for him to fall asleep when he gets back to his apartment, thoughts of home supplant those of the afterschool kids. A nursing gig. Picking up the financial advisor basics from Bill. But as soon as his feet touch his bike pedals and he rides past the rec center in the morning, those dreams dissipate like phantoms trapped inside the warehouse.

During a pick-up game on the day before his flight home, five men strut in through a side door that leads directly into the gym. They're wet from spring drizzle. Their shoes squeak, smear mud. One, in a baseball cap and winter jacket, glares at Connor. All are silent, except for a nineteen-year-old named Keon, who puts his hands up and backs away from them, shouting, "No, no, no, no, no."

The intruders surround him under the basket and escort him back toward the door, one of them shoving him from behind. Momentarily shocked, three of the basketball players, topless, wearing oversized gym shorts, run after the men, and the group slips out into the rain.

The door closes behind them, and Connor looks at the mud on the floor, then at the anxious few left in the gym. They scratch their chests and stretch their legs, avoiding one another's eyes.

"What the fuck was that about?" Connor asks.

They say nothing and he runs out of the gym toward the front desk. "These guys just took Keon," he tells Danielle, who's sitting on the hallway bench reading a children's book to Marquees. "They just, like, grabbed him and left. Where's EJ?"

"In the office."

She stands, holding the boy, and looks past his shoulder through the glass front door. Connor turns and watches Keon and the five men walk toward a house across the street. They back Keon against the slate-concrete retaining wall of the house's steep front lawn, and he casually sits on the wall, as if he doesn't mind their company.

Connor steps toward the door, but Danielle grabs a fistful of the back of his shirt.

Keon hardly defends himself, so the men don't need to hold him down. The man in the hat and coat starts punching him, first in the chest, then in the face, shoving him back against the muddy slope every time he tries to sit up. The three basketball players stand around them, shouting and threatening to intervene, but they don't. The man puts his knee on Keon's chest to keep him still, then cocks his shoulder, raises his fist, and strikes again and again.

Connor reaches back to free his shirt. "I won't go. I won't go," he tells her. "What is this? What's going on? Why...?"

Danielle releases him. The man suddenly stops throwing punches and reaches into his waistband, and the players take off down the street. The guys from the gym now crowd the desk, watching Keon. One of them presses his nose against the front door, his hands on his head. They all wait for the man to pull out his gun and kill Keon. EJ stands in front of Connor, watching and waiting, too, until Danielle picks him up with her free arm and carries the two boys into the gym. Then the man with the cap removes his empty hand from his waistband, and suddenly the street is empty, aside from Keon slouched on the curb, his back to the wall.

Two hours later, after Keon's friends take him to his mom's, only Connor, Danielle, Marquees, and EJ remain. Connor mops up the mud on the court, then sits alone beneath the hoop, his arms stretched out, elbows on his knees.

When EJ and Marquees come in to run laps around the edges of the basketball court, Connor lies on his back and reaches for their legs as they scamper past. They giggle louder with every lap. He stands and they jump on him and hang on his neck and shoulders. When he doesn't try to wriggle free, they beg him to. "Come on. Come on. Just one time," EJ says.

He does, just once, moving in exaggerated slow-motion and groaning like a monster. "I should keep cleaning," he tells them.

They continue running laps while he vacuums the dried mud in the hallway and Danielle stands over the office desk, prepping snacks for the afterschool kids. She pours pretzels into plastic baggies, which she seals and tosses into a bright green tub. As he puts the vacuum away in the nearby utility closet, she says, "The kids say you like me." He frowns at her, and when neither speaks, he finishes putting the vacuum away in the closet and closes the door, as if he didn't hear her. "You've never seen a beating before."

"Not like that," he says.

"Could've been a lot worse. None of them were carrying."

"How could you tell?"

She looks over at him. "You look like you saw a ghost."

"I'm mad."

"Right. Me too. But no one's an angel. Not Keon. And there's nothing to do about it, even if he was."

"That's callous."

She nods. "Did you hear me, about the kids?"

He glances down the hallway to make sure they're alone, then he sits on the front desk. "What did I do? Which kids?"

"All of them."

"What is it? Boyfriend going to kill me?"

"*I'll* kill you."

"That's fair."

"I know it's fair," she replies.

"We could be friends, you know."

"I'll think about it."

"That's fair."

"I know it is."

"What are you doing on the computer all the time?" he asks.

"Nothing."

"Fine. No, I've never seen that type of thing with Keon. What was that about?"

"Don't know."

"You do, though. You know everything, so what does it matter what the kids tell you?"

The tub of pretzels swooshes as she carries it out of the office and drops it next to him. In her narrowed olive eyes are streaks of auburn and crimson. He looks away from them to put the plastic lid on the tub. He rests the tub on his lap and lifts his gaze again to find that she's still glaring at him, her cheeks livid.

"You're a tourist," she says. "You're visiting. It's a vacation for you."

"I like it here."

"And when you stop liking it, you'll leave. These kids can't. I can't. It's only going to get harder for you here. Harder to stay, harder to go."

"Why do you say that?"

She holds her hands out and he gives her the tub. "You know what I mean," she says.

"You *want* me to leave so you can say you were right about me."

"I *am* right."

Hopping down from the desk, he says, "What if I'm not the asshole you want me to be?"

"Never said you were."

The boys' screeches echo in the hallway as they run toward her. EJ grabs one of her thighs, Marquees the other. Connor makes a silly face at them and they laugh.

"I never said that," she continues, smiling politely at Connor in front of her nephews. "I said you're a tourist."

Mid-morning, Connor spots Bill in the pick-up area adjacent to the last baggage carousel at the Minneapolis airport. His back to the entrance, Bill leans against the hood of his recently washed black BMW, chatting up one of the security guards. In beige khakis and a sunflower-yellow golfer's polo accentuating the tan back of his neck, Bill small talks his way into loitering in the tow-away zone. As the bulky, uniformed thirty-something with an amber goatee nods along, Connor imagines his father's embrace, but also the fallout of booking the next flight back to Chicago, claiming that mechanical issues rerouted him to Milwaukee and he therefore couldn't make it north.

When Connor interrupts their conversation about "mutual fund diversification," the guard scowls at him. "Don't listen to this small-time hustler," Connor tells him.

Beaming, Bill turns, his dimples shadowy, brown hair neatly trimmed, and gray eyes sleek and lustrous as his car. He grabs his son—the strength of his lean, bronzed arms startling Connor—and pecks his cheeks. After another firm hug, Connor backs away, wipes his cheek on the shoulder of his shirt. Bill introduces him to the guard, to whom he hands a business card before slipping into the leather seat next to Connor.

Connor examines his father's fresh-from-the-box white golfing shoes, as Bill shuts the door and says, "They expect you to drive around in circles while you wait. To hell with that."

"What are you wearing?"

Bill pulls thin-framed sunglasses from the breast pocket of his polo, puts them on with both hands, and pops a stick of gum in his mouth.

"What a douche."

"Seems like a nice guy."

"Not him. You trying out for the Senior PGA Tour?"

Bill looks at himself in the rearview mirror. With his left hand on the wheel, he reaches over to clutch the back of Connor's neck. He glances at Connor's torn jeans and faded white muscle shirt. "Well…you look like the drummer in a garage band. And nobody wants to come to your shows because you guys suck. How's that?"

"You got me."

Minneapolis is sunny and hot. Bill turns on the air conditioning and starts to drive. "Jesus, I missed you. Every time you don't answer your phone, I imagine you've been shot." Bill puts both hands on the wheel. "I want you to meet some people while you're here."

"Charlotte."

"Not just her. You didn't make plans for today, did you?"

"When did you start golfing?" Connor asks.

"I've always loved golf."

"You've never even owned clubs."

"Always wanted to, though."

"Charlotte must like it," Connor says.

"Mr. Nicholson does, her dad. I want you to meet him. He's a broker. Retired now. But he was high up once upon a time. Really smart guy. I've been playing with him. It's embarrassing for me because I'm all sweaty after three holes. But Mr. Nicholson is in great shape for an older guy. The barrel-chested type. He used to play linebacker at Wisconsin, if you can believe that. You never see him breathing heavily. Meanwhile, I'm huffing and puffing. It's mortifying. Another thing—he drinks like a fish. Well, he's retired. You're going to meet him. You have to. Him and Charlotte, of course."

"Spending a lot of time with him, huh?"

"I'm enjoying it."

"Something's up with you. Too much coffee, maybe."

"I'm just glad to be with you."

"You're trying to set me up with a job here, aren't you?" Connor shakes his head and looks out his window. "Unreal. I bet this broker guy has a temp job ready for me. I bet his office is a block from yours."

"You caught me. Yep, I started seeing Charlotte just to score you a sweet entry-level position. It was a long con, but the jig is finally up. Can you walk nine holes in those shoes?"

"Don't get your hopes up. I'm going back in a few days no matter what."

"Need money?"

"I need a cigarette."

"Smoke a cigar with Mr. Nicholson. How are things with Vanessa? She says you're being distant."

"I am distant. So, we're golfing?"

"If you're up for it. What's going on with you? You okay?"

Connor nods, scratches his shaved chin.

"Work's been insane," Bill says. "I don't know when it'll calm down. My clients are losing their minds with the market dropping. They blame me for everything, too, even though I lose just like they do. Not as bad as some people, but I lose. If I knew what was going to happen ahead of time, I'd warn everyone. Well, if I knew, I wouldn't be a small-time hustler, like you say. You read the newspaper."

"Your clients are lucky to have something to lose. The kids at the center have real problems. It's not lost-my-boat-have-to-spend-a-few-more-years-at-the-office shit. It's stuff I couldn't have imagined before, most of it. You wouldn't believe me if I told you."

"You're tough now, huh?"

Connor shrugs. "I didn't say that."

"Everybody has struggles and tragedy, Connor. Even well-off people."

"Like picking out the right polo to impress your father-in-law with?"

"Don't be like that. Don't be cruel."

Connor shakes his head. They drive in silence for a few highway miles.

"Anyway, yes, it took me a long time to pick out this shirt.

Before you get all moody and run off again, can I tell you some good news?"

"Go ahead."

"Connor."

He looks over at Bill, who tilts his head down and looks over his glasses at his son. Bill softens his voice. "You have no idea, huh? Charlotte and I are...we're serious. Before you say something about things moving too quickly, just meet her." He glances back and forth between the road and his son's stunned expression. When Connor says nothing, Bill begins to sputter. "You'll understand better when you get older. I'm never going to get swept away like I was with your mom. It won't happen...and I'm fine with that. And Charlotte and I wanted to take it slow, but..."

"I'm happy for you," Connor says, mercifully. "I'm glad. It's a good thing. Just surprised. When do I meet her?"

Bill lifts his eyebrows, draws a deep breath, and checks his watch. "She's teeing off with us in fifteen minutes."

At the country-club pro shop, Bill buys Connor a white shirt with the club logo stitched on the breast, two crossed putters circled. Connor puts it on over his shirt. "I look like a caddy," he says. "Why didn't you tell me we were golfing?"

"Thought you might not come."

"Good point."

They walk through the club restaurant to the back patio, where the aroma of newly cut grass marinates the brunch hour. The seating area is divided in half by a series of concrete landings that descend to the first hole's tee box. Umbrellas shade the many tables on each side. Wispy, unspooling clouds reveal the gaudy sun inching toward high noon and brushing aside the last of the course shadows.

A canvas tent awning, the sandy brown hue of which matches that of the siding, shades a long bar area on the first landing. There, atop barstools sit eight men in front of eight thick Bloody Marys. The man on the far stool stands mid-swig and walks over to greet Bill and Connor.

James Nicholson is tall and stout. He wears shiny black golf shoes, white pants, a black belt, and a tucked-in emerald shirt. With a full head of coiffed silver hair, he looks like a retired athlete at a charity event. When he smiles, his mouth seems large enough to swallow a softball.

After introductions, he downs the rest of his drink in three gulps, sticks the four-inch toothpick of skewered pickles and olives into his mouth, and pulls the toothpick out clean. Then he tosses his golf bag on his back and points to the first hole fifty yards away. In the rough beside the tee box, a woman takes practices swings.

"She's waiting for us," he says, his voice resonant, gruff. Leading them down the landings and onto the lawn, he says to Connor, "Your dad told me you're working down in Chicago. Mentioned you might be interested in something local, something that pays a little better than what you're getting. If you'd like, I'll contact some old colleagues at the office. Otherwise, I'm sure one of the guys up at the bar could get you an interview somewhere. Let me know if you're interested."

Gazing at the distant first hole, Bill avoids Connor's stare. "Thanks," Connor replies. "I'll keep that in mind, Mr. Nicholson."

"Call me James."

"His office was downtown," Bill explains. "About twenty minutes from mine. We used to play softball with the men in the corporate law offices on the floor just below his."

"You golf, Connor?" James asks.

"Not really, no."

"Maybe you'll make your dad's game look not so awful. Have a drink with me," James commands him, waving at the passing drink cart. "Don't worry about money, either. Everything's free today."

A college girl in a tank top and short skirt pulls up in the cart, fixes them each a Bloody Mary in a plastic cup. James hands her a twenty, tells her to keep the change, and introduces her to Connor. "Katie, I can tell you right now that this guy's going to be very successful. Trust me. A damn good-looking fellow, too, I'd say."

Connor takes his drink from Katie. Her cheeks glisten with sweat as she smiles at him. When she drives off, James says, "Don't worry. There's dozens of girls just like that here. We'll see her again, too."

"Thanks for the drink."

"She's cute, huh?"

"I have a girlfriend."

"No crime in not telling Katie about her right away. No crime."

James swallows an inch of his drink, then bites down on the cup, freeing his hands to search the pouches of his golf bag for balls.

Connor turns his cup in the sunlight; it's so strong, it looks like grapefruit juice with a half-inch of vodka on top. "You don't skimp on the liquor here," he says.

"Like I told you, everything's free. Got cigars for us later, too."

As they walk toward the tee box, Connor looks out over the expanse of kempt, pampered grass. High schoolers and Hispanic men in cardboard-brown pullovers rake bunkers and trim hedges at the fringes of the nearby driving range. Trust fund preppy boys weave golf carts along the paved trails at the fairway edges. He tips his cup back for a sip, then finishes the rest like he's taking a shot. The vodka dazes him. He rattles the ice inside his cup, clears his throat, and fingers loose the pickle at the bottom before munching it down. After flipping the ice into the rough, he glances up and discovers that the woman waiting for them is younger and more striking than the one he anticipated meeting. Behind a red visor, a braid of biscuit-blonde hair falls between her shoulder blades. She turns and starts toward him. She wears shorts, pink golf shoes, and a sleeveless white polo against which her teal eyes cut. Preparing to shake her hand, he wipes the pickle juice from his fingertips onto his pant leg, but she lunges forward and hugs him.

"Sorry, I'm a little sweaty. It's so good to meet you," she says, holding him at arm's length, a hand on each shoulder, and examining his facial features, then Bill's. "I can see it in the shape of your noses and cheeks. Both of you are so handsome." She releases his shoulders and they walk toward the first tee. "Connor, I'm going to apologize in advance for anything my dad says today. He's argumentative and opinionated. He's a bully and he's always been that way."

James huffs and chuckles. "She's right—I *am* a bully. But I'm also a good time, and we're going to enjoy ourselves today," he replies, flagging down the next drink cart.

Between holes, James and Connor swap empty cups for full ones and James introduces him to dutifully flirty cart girls. He watches as James criticizes Bill's swing, lambasts Bill's taste in cigars, evangelizes for Bill, louder the more lubricated he grows, the "miracles" of his portfolio maneuvers, leveraging his self-perceived advantages over Bill in a game about which no one but James cares. Connor notes the mirth in Charlotte's eyes as they pounce between the three men, the tomboyish way she thumbs the collar of her polo to her temples when dabbing up sweat droplets. He listens as she and Bill relay the details of how they met: the yoga studio above a Chinese restaurant, the swelter and stink of their Super-Cardio classes, the trainer's comically arrhythmic instructions, the bloody steaks and Malbec, the North Shore weekend, the happy hour margaritas with her coworkers, the European heritage tour travel plans.

Connor's drunk crests when he stains his pant leg maroon with the cup he knows is one too many. He orders two more, slugs his way into knee-deep foliage in search of an errant ball, and there, as the heat overwhelms him, loses himself in thought, belches, and pours both cups out.

On the final hole, James, with a six-stroke lead, philosophizes on the economy, pausing only when one of them is about to swing. Connor grits his teeth.

"Allow me to be flippant with you, Connor. I'll start with the basics. Somewhere along the line, Americans, the most ignorant people in the world, got it in their heads that everyone is entitled to everything all the time. American dream, American dream, and all that horseshit. Houses, boats, cars, cabins, vacations, and so on. Americans buy and buy and buy, and the prices of what they're buying keep rising and rising and rising. What's it all based on? A dream. America sells the dream to the middle class. Banks issue dream loans. Wall Street buys the dream and dresses it up and sells it to investors, who then sell the dream to those handling the middle classes' pensions and 401(k)s and so on and so on...So, what's the issue? When the market is soaring, and everyone's getting wealthy and going to bed every night with their dream, what's the problem? Well, the dream isn't real. You see, Connor?"

"Yep."

"Every day, tens of millions of Americans buy things they can't afford so that tens of millions of Americans can have more money to spend on things they can't afford. But what happens when the economy contracts and the cash stops flowing? When banks won't issue loans? When investors are skittish and Wall Street begins to check on its cash reserves? When the pensioners hide in government bonds? Well, that's precisely when the dreamers must, again, double down on their dreams. No?"

"Got it."

"Because we're not all losers, Connor. Some of us make out extremely well. Suppose you put six hundred thousand of the bank's funny-money into a few different houses, did some standard upkeep, and sold them off just before the mortgage crisis took the economy down. What, then?"

Connor stares down at his ball, wiggling his shoulders and hips as he imagines he should, and mutters, "You'd make a lot of money."

Charlotte says, "Connor, you don't have to humor him. You won't hurt his self-confidence, believe me."

Connor shrugs, graciously smiles at her, and swings. The short drive slices slightly but stays on the fairway. He pulls his tee from the ground, steps off the box.

James places his ball on a tee, then stands, gazing down the fairway at Connor's drive. Admiring his club, he squares himself to the ball, all the while sermonizing. "Connor, you can drive the ball farther than that. Looks like the little guy's getting tired. Maybe he's too skinny for these drinks. Don't worry, we're almost done. Anyway, like I've been trying to tell you, the world's a jungle. We tell ourselves we live in civilization. Skyscrapers and medical devices. We don't. We live in the jungle. Ultimately, it's a battle between men. Sorry, Charlotte, you know what I mean. It's the will of the survivor, one man against the other. Darwinism, all that. I know what you're thinking, too, Connor. Some people have bad schools, bad parents, drugs, economic problems, health problems. Some will lose out when the housing market crashes, for example, even though they took out responsible loans. I'm sure you've seen it where you're living."

James freezes at the top of his backswing, his colossal brawn poised, then rips the ball off the tee. He watches the ball outdrive Connor's and land near the lip of the green, then bends to pluck his unscathed tee, which he pins between his teeth. He steps off the tee box, leans against his club, and pulls the tee from his mouth. "But, tell me, how is that different than a kid getting leukemia? I'd even argue that nature is more merciful than the market. She makes it quick and easy, most of the time; there's no safety net when it comes to bad genes. What do you say, Connor? Bill? A jungle, no?"

"I suppose we make our own paths in life," Bill replies. "Have to be responsible for ourselves."

Connor glances at Bill, who's preparing to tee off. Sweat dribbles down the sides of Bill's face. Staring down, he pauses longer than he has before any shot today, then hooks the ball into the trees separating their fairway from an adjacent one.

"Even for you, that was lousy, Bill," James says.

Bill wipes his face with a towel, smiles, and says, "Looks like I'll take last again. At least the pressure's off now."

James looks him over. "Anyway, like I was saying—"

"We get your point, Dad," Charlotte says. "You're a big shot."

"I don't know if you do. See, it's a jungle, Charlotte. Some of us are lions ripping up our portions of the carcass."

They wait as Bill uses three strokes to hit his ball back onto the fairway and up onto the green, where James continues. "Now, to be honest with you, I just can't muster all that much sympathy for folks who dream too much, get carried away, and lose out. Connor, you're young. You probably remember the last time you went to the zoo and saw the lion in his cage. You think he has sympathy for what he kills? You think he cares about how weak or injured or slow his prey is? The lion just gets hungry, and then what, Connor?"

Connor squats in front of his ball, eyeing the slope of the green before him as he imagines he should. He glares up at Bill and says, "He eats."

"That's exactly right, son," James replies.

Bill, forty feet from the flag, strikes his ball and yells, "Shit! Too hard!" Then he watches as it closes in on the hole, clangs against the post, and vanishes. He holds his putter above his head like a rifleman wading across a river. "Shot of the day!" he cries as Charlotte hugs him.

The shot does not alter James' smug grin. He puffs his chest out, spits in the grass, and buries his short putt to finish the day at par. After Connor two-putts to end his half-round, James slaps him on the back and, looking down at him, bares his teeth and roars teasingly. Then he chuckles and says, "It's all fun. I hardly listen to myself when I talk, anyway. Good round. Sure you don't play much?"

"Thanks for letting me join you."

"Of course. There's prime rib waiting for us up at the clubhouse. Who's ready for lunch?"

On the walk back, Connor and Charlotte lag behind, heavy with perspiration.

Quietly, she says, "You have no idea how much I hate golf."

"I think I do. My dad hates golf, too. Probably hasn't told you that."

"He pretends well," she says. "By the way, my dad doesn't believe everything he says."

"Mine doesn't say everything he believes."

"Since retirement, Dad's looking for an argument, a little excitement. Ignore him if you can."

"He's fine."

"Your girlfriend's wonderful. We had dinner with her last week." She whispers, "I didn't tell your dad this, but she told me you're considering coming back very soon."

"No. I have too much going on back home."

"Enjoying your work?"

"Other things, mostly. The rec center. I know I could volunteer anywhere, but I've been gone for almost a year now and I'm starting to build roots."

"Your dad might not tell you this enough, but he's extremely proud of you. You're doing things your own way. I find it inspiring. A lot of people wait too long in life to figure out who they are. You must be mature beyond your years."

"Must be," Connor replies.

"Tell me more about the center."

Connor talks about the kids and the guys he plays basketball with. He tells her about Lee, but only after she promises not to mention him to Bill.

Back at the restaurant, a reserved patio table adorned with two bottles of red wine awaits them. The lunch crowd fills the other tables, the women in sundresses or blazers, the men in suits or golfing attire. As all but James take their seats in the shade of their table's umbrella, many in the crowd wave and smile at him. One reminds him of a bet they made on the NBA finals, another tells him to come over soon for some fifty-year-old Japanese whiskey. When James disappears into the clubhouse to peruse his humidor for cigars, Bill and Charlotte examine the reds on the table, confirming what they learned in a recent wine tasting.

"Red wine has more tannins, doesn't it?" she asks.

"Yes, and Merlot comes from the Bordeaux," he replies. "If I remember correctly, I liked the more acidic grapes."

"Acidic grapes?" Connor says to Bill, incredulous. "You've never been interested in wine."

"It's something to do with the aftertaste. And, yes, I have."

Connor rubs his sore jaw, wonders how long he's been gritting his teeth. A waitress places a glass of water in front of him and he gulps it down.

James returns with two forty-gauge cigars, hands one to Connor, and lights them both with one match. He insists on Connor having a "real man's lunch," prime rib and asparagus, while Bill and Charlotte order a flatbread with vinaigrette, arugula, and prosciutto, and gush about their summer plans to kayak in the Boundary Waters and road-trip to Napa Valley. Connor drinks two glasses of wine before his food arrives, at times giddy, at times queasy, at times scornful. He accidentally burns his wrist with his cigar, then looks around to ensure no one saw him. James orders the table another bottle.

As they eat, James begins to describe his financial goals for the next four years, then suddenly addresses Connor, "But please, please, please let me know what I can do for you. Your dad says you're in a tough place there in Chicago, pulling in minimum wage. That won't do, I promise you. I can square you up, make it right. Only if you're interested, of course. I'll get you set up, licensed, and making six figures in less than eighteen months. Any time. Charlotte will give you my number."

Connor narrows his eyes at him and nods. "I've been thinking. If we were a nation of laws, we could have a free market. But we're not, so we don't. The poor and the middle class have laws, sure, but the rich live without them. And since I doubt any of these career criminals at the top will spend a day behind bars for what they do, I'll tell you what I think should happen to them—"

"Connor, it's only conversation," Bill interjects.

"Here's *my* dream," Connor continues, still eyeing James. "We take the bankers who push predatory loans on widows and working-class families, and the inside traders and shady offshore investment brokers..."

"Connor..." Bill whispers.

Connor points his cigar, like a dart, at James' face. "...no messy trials, no lawyers, no plea deals, no community service..."

James is grinning now, feigning amusement in an attempt to conceal his reddening cheeks.

"Connor, it's just conversation," Bill says.

The tip of Connor's cigar sizzles when he stabs it into the bottom of his empty wineglass. He stands. His head swirling, he clutches his cloth napkin, steadies himself on the back of his chair, and swallows hard.

"You won't let me respond?" James says, dumbfounded, looking at Connor, then at a shocked but entertained Charlotte, then at a mortified Bill.

"No," Connor replies. "But thank you for lunch."

Dropping the napkin on his chair, he snatches the remaining hunk of meat from his plate and saunters up the landings and into the clubhouse, savoring the last morsels. One of the bartenders points him to the bathroom, cool and pristine and sprawling, smelling of lavender and potpourri, where he throws away his sweaty pro-shop shirt, ducks into the first stall, and vomits into the toilet.

Connor sleeps on the ride home, then showers, stumbles to his bedroom, strips down to his boxers, and takes a brief, fidgety afternoon nap from which Vanessa wakes him with a thudding flick on his forehead. "Who's Carol?" she says, sitting on his bed.

Groggy, still drunk, he replies, "Who's *who*?"

She tosses his phone on his chest and he looks at a text from Lee's friend Carol: *lee fell off a roof at work. broke his legs all over. shits bad here*

She says, "Didn't want to snoop. Just saw the name. I also see that you've been getting my calls."

"Lee got hurt."

"The addict?"

He looks up at her. She wears a sage dress and silk scarf. Her hair, newly highlighted toffee-blonde, is in a bun on the back of her head and her eyelashes are lined with mascara. Against her tan, her scar is blunter than usual.

"You look beautiful."

"We need to talk about when you're having dinner with my parents like you promised."

"So beautiful."

Looking away, she heaves a theatrical sigh. "Your dad said you made an ass of yourself today."

"Last thing I remember, he was glaring at me in the rear-view mirror. Heat got to me."

"Maybe *you* got to you. Did you brush your teeth?"

"Many times."

She draws her legs up onto the bed and crawls toward him. She whispers in his ear, "He went out to pick up pizza." They kiss and he pulls the straps of her dress off her shoulders. As she hikes her dress up to her hips, he begins to fully wake, places his hands on her shoulders. "What?" she asks, nibbling his clavicle. When he doesn't reply, she bites him. She sits up, grips the bunched hem of her dress.

"That hurt." He glowers at her, his hands on her smooth, bronzed thighs.

She clears her throat to rid her voice of grievance, as though he were incapable of hurting her. "What's going on?" she asks.

"I'm sorry."

"You're still drunk. How about I leave before you say more?"

"I've slept it off. Honestly, I *am* sorry to do things this way. I've been stupid about so much. And you're such an awesome girl."

"Fuck off."

Brushing down his bedhead, he says, "I'm not coming back to Minneapolis. I like what I have going on."

"No, you don't. You're just being contrary. If Chicago loved you as much as we do here, you wouldn't want to be there either."

"I'm sorry."

"I believe you. You know you'll regret this, and that you're going to do it anyway is the most fucked-up part. You're ruining what you have for no reason. I'm beginning to remember why things didn't work out between us in college," she says.

"Don't make this a huge thing. In a few months you'll meet some great guy—"

"Such a frightened boy, like you've been all along," she snaps.

"Vanessa…"

She pulls the straps of her dress up on her shoulders. The hem tumbles to her ankles when she stands to exit the room. "Tell your dad I feel bad I can't have pizza tonight."

She slams the door behind her.

Unable to fall asleep, he throws on gym shorts and explores the empty house's new décor, which he immediately realizes Charlotte has managed to transform while living, Bill claims, in an apartment downtown. Fresh flowers grace the living room TV stand, the bathrooms, and the kitchen table and counter. The pantry wine rack is stocked. Fresh fruits and vegetables ornament the kitchen's island counter, where an assortment of certified organic African and South American whole beans surrounds the coffeemaker. A breeze traipsing through the living room window rustles the newspaper on the coffee table, the sections of which someone, presumably Charlotte, separated and artfully arranged in the shape of a diamond.

Though it's almost dinnertime, he makes a pot of coffee and searches the master bedroom upstairs for the pack of smokes Bill invariably hid in his sock drawer when Connor lived at home. Connor is annoyed, then, to discover only men's and women's socks in the drawer, and becomes progressively aggravated as he forages the house's many nooks—the guest bathroom vanity, the loose ceiling tiles in Bill's walk-in closet, the shadowy recesses of the cubbies in the den desk—without success. Eventually, he discovers the smokes in a shoebox under the sink and steps out onto the back porch with the newspaper, a cup of coffee, and a cigarette that tastes like dirt laced with cleaning powder. On a shaded lawn chair facing the glass door to the house, he smokes and reads and sips his sobering coffee. Soon, however, entranced by the details of a recent US drone strike in the Middle East, he slouches and begins to doze off, elbows on the arms of the chair, smoke slithering up beside him.

When Bill bursts through the door with a pizza box, Connor wakes, takes a deep drag, and exhales.

"Don't act like you enjoyed that. Those taste like shit," Bill says. "Come in for pizza."

They sit on the burgundy leather couch in the living room, watching but not paying attention to the evening news on the TV in front of them.

"House looks different," Connor says. "There are air fresheners in the bathroom. Smells like apricots everywhere."

"You like her?"

"I like her a lot. Her dad's a knuckle-dragger, though."

"He kind of is. But last winter, he made fifty grand in one weekend of trading. Where's Vanessa?"

"We broke up."

Bill stares at Connor, who fakes interest in a prescription drug commercial, then slumps into the cushion. "When did this happen?"

"Hour ago."

"Vanessa was wonderful for you. You've behaved like a real jerk this whole day."

"I'm having a good time."

"She was a great girl."

"She's not dead."

"Connor, I wish I could bite my tongue, but I really think you should come home and get your life together. First off,

Charlotte's dad buys you lunch, a cigar, and enough booze to kill a buffalo. How do you repay him? You get snippy with him. Tell him, basically, that you wish he were dead."

"You act like I need an intervention because I broke up with my girlfriend. You're being childish."

"*I'm* not the one who threw up in public today."

"Well...actually, you've got me there."

"Connor, you really need to consider coming back. I think it'd do you good."

"I'm sorry about today. But you're being ridiculous."

They watch the rest of the news in silence.

"So, you like her, huh?"

Connor looks Bill over. "I do. Don't fuck it up."

"I'll try not to."

Under the guise of getting them ice cream for dessert, Connor takes the BMW for an hour-long drive north of Minneapolis, stopping to fill the gas tank at a station near the Albertville mall and walking along the storefront boulevards that seem to have no end. He texts friends from college to let them know he's in town, Danielle to ask about Keon. She replies that he's recovering well. Connor thinks better of texting her anything else. He passes obnoxious high school girls carrying colorful, oversized shopping bags, men with gelled hair picking up newly tailored suits, and couples playing footsie at sidewalk tables in front of cafés. He thinks about Danielle. On the drive home, his college roommate Chad invites him to a party the following night.

Connor stays up late watching TV and sleeps until the following afternoon, when Bill takes him to the Mall of America for lunch and tries to buy him some collared shirts.

"I can't wear these," Connor tells him.

"You're too proud."

"No, really, Dad. The kids will laugh at me."

Eventually he settles for new socks and underwear. "Souvenirs," Bill calls them.

As night approaches, Connor cleans up and borrows a black sport coat and dress shoes from Bill. An Uber takes him to an Edina house with a convoluted patchwork of eaves and a squat spire over the porch, and he walks to a fenced-in backyard that smells of damp cedar. There is a firepit, a creaky wooden swing, a gazebo, and two dozen people he knows from college. Chad, tall and already slurring-drunk, side-hugs him, pulls him in for a kiss on the cheek, and leads him to a gazebo bench.

"I heard a lot of shit about you," Chad shouts. "You were dead. Then you were in China, hooking up with all sorts of Chinese girls. Then you were backpacking in the Ozarks. Then you were on heroin. Then Vanessa told me you two were hooking up in Chicago. You look good. I heard you're starting med school next year. You should. It's badass, man."

Connor drinks a beer, peeling the label away as Chad tells him about his dreams of becoming a widely respected gastrointestinal surgeon, then having a three-way with two of his med school professors.

When the son of the homeowners, an unemployed environmental studies major who goes by Bruce G., finishes showing off the cedar fence his father paid him to build, he gives Connor directions to the basement in case Connor wants some coke. After lamenting to some girls the effects of climate change on Sub-Saharan Africa, Bruce slips a joint into the inner breast pocket of Connor's coat and sings, "First one's free, on the G. First one's free, on the G," shimmying, his hands above his head.

There are dapper East Coast professionals who flew in just for the night, and painters, cooks, and grocery store clerks who graduated with honors a year ago. Connor listens to their conversations. Their parents mean well but take no responsibility for raping the world. The soldiers need to come home from the Middle East. The ice caps are melting.

Connor drinks another beer and wanders over to the fire, where a girl is playing dance music on her cellphone. A woman in a short tangerine dress, whom Connor doesn't recognize, takes him by the hand and dances with him in the firelight that, as she turns, exposes the sweat melting her makeup away from her brow. When she grinds up against him, he steps away, and Chad grabs her by the wrist and leads her into the house, spanking her as he opens the door for her. She giggles. Connor sits on a stump and eyes the fire for half an hour, then he hands his joint to the girl next to him, orders an Uber, and leaves without saying goodbye to anyone.

At home he lies in the front lawn, his father's coat folded next to him. He drafts texts to Danielle but doesn't send them. When the kitchen light turns on, he watches Charlotte, in shorts and a hooded sweatshirt, set her laptop up next to the coffeemaker on the island and begin to type, stopping every so often to sip her beer.

She catches sight of him as he's walking toward the door, waves, and closes her computer. He pours himself a glass of water, sits down at an island stool across from her, and apologizes for lunch. "It was cool of your dad to treat us."

"You don't have to be nice, Connor."

"He talks too much, in that case."

"I'm used to it."

"Thought you were a wine person," he says, nodding at her beer.

She scrunches her nose up, shrugs. "I like trying new things. I also do a lot of things I don't like and have never liked. I hate golf. I hate meetings. I hate being around Scotch and cigars. I hate men. In fact, I don't like most people, if I'm being honest."

"You like anything?"

She tips her beer back, replies, "I like your dad."

"My dad never told me what you do."

"I'm a marketing consultant. A matchmaker. I help businesses find their customers. I like it, but what I'm most interested in is helping young women get into business, networking with the colleges and universities in Minnesota to encourage talented girls to join the business community. As you can imagine, we're underrepresented. So, I speak on panels and make contacts. These girls don't want to play golf and listen to men explain things they already understand, and if there are enough women pulling the strings in the future, they won't have to. So that's that. Tell me more about Chicago."

She finishes her beer and grabs another. He scratches his neck.

"I bike and play basketball, and I used to have a neighbor who was interesting but I haven't seen him for a while. Apparently, he just broke his legs. I told you about him already." He pauses, grimaces wryly at his own words. "Chicago kind of sucks, actually. I mean, what I have going on isn't what I'd hoped for." He finishes his glass of water. "But I did meet this woman."

"Not Vanessa?"

"No. She has a boyfriend; I don't think she's married. She works where I volunteer."

"Does she like you?"

"No," he replies. "Definitely not."

"Maybe she will."

"I doubt it."

He closes his eyes as though to fall asleep on the stool.

"Bill wanted me to talk to you, which I thought was a silly idea because we've only just met, of course. Please don't tell him I came clean with this, but I had this whole speech planned for you, for his sake. I'm embarrassed now to admit it."

"Let me hear it."

She laughs.

"You wouldn't have brought it up if you didn't want to say it."

"Hold on." After finishing her beer, she looks at him, laughs again, then straightens her face. "*Connor*...I'm nervous now... *You really seem like a good kid*...Jesus, that's corny... *Bill tells me you left Minneapolis because you were disillusioned about medical school and you wanted to discover your own way. I've been a corporate professional for almost ten years, so I can tell you that you're right to believe that wherever there's power to be had, there are unfeeling and selfish people, and you're likely to end up working for and with them. But, in my opinion, it doesn't serve the world to hide from moving up in life, through school or employment or whatever, because positions of power are those most in need of good and caring people.*"

He waits for her to finish before laughing. "Sounds like something from a commencement address," he says, wiping tears from his eyes.

"Not bad, huh?"

"I shouldn't laugh; my dad's going mental over all this. He's got you lobbying for my return like I'm a political prisoner."

"He loves you."

"I know, I know."

She taps her bottle on the island. After a minute she says, "I don't think you should come home now. Not just because of the woman, either. What's her name?"

"Danielle."

"Not just because of Danielle. You have an itch to scratch, otherwise you wouldn't have left in the first place. Easy for me to tell you; I don't miss you all the time like he does."

He stares at his glass, then walks to the sink to fill it. "My dad said you have an apartment."

"I do, sometimes," she replies cheekily.

As he leaves the kitchen, she opens her laptop and begins typing again.

❧

Summer heat cauterizes Chicago. When it rains, the kids in Connor's apartment complex play tag in the courtyard down the street, kicking puddle water at one another, balling their clothes into sopping wads and firing them at passing cars; he lounges on the landing steps, baptized in the sky's acidic mercy. Every morning, after the night's dispossessed shelter themselves in shaded alley crannies, and before the day's assume their posts on back stoops and slanted benches, he runs eight miles. The web of jutting side streets and rambling neighborhoods reveals itself to him in quarter-mile increments—the houses in which the rec center kids live, the buildings in which their parents and step-parents and grandparents work; the rusted steel girders of railway bridges; the parched communal gardens; immense slopes stippled with trash; brick walls graffitied with symbols and images seemingly from another language; the church in which someone shoots up, the bedroom in which he prays.

After, he stretches in the kitchen; his sweat trickles onto the linoleum. He showers and sleeps, then goes to the center, where the other men no longer abuse him during pickup games on the outdoor gravel courts, where the schoolkids hang from his sturdy sunburned arms and take turns scuffing up the new running shoes Bill insisted on mailing him.

"You're not special, man," Lee says, lying on the squeaky cot Carol lent Connor. Lee wears a sleeveless undershirt translucent with sweat, his legs propped up on a milk crate Connor found in the building's dumpster, his soft-casts on the floor.

Connor stands over him. "You should wear those casts."

"Too hot. I can't sleep. The doctor said to sleep."

"She also said you should wear your casts so your ankles don't heal all fucked up. You want clubfoot?"

"Used to have clubfoot every Friday and Saturday night."

"Good one."

"Shit hurts too bad."

Connor lets Lee stay with him rent-free under two conditions: Lee can't bring drugs into the house and Connor must administer the pain pills, which he stores in the cupboard above the fridge. Lee fusses but, with no other options, would've conceded much more.

"What were you doing on the roof?"

"Howling at the moon, fuck you mean. I was getting back to work. What are you still doing here?"

"I'll figure something out."

"You been here a year already, haven't learned shit," Lee says, sipping water from a giant straw, a sixty-four ounce gas station mug tucked in his armpit. "You must be getting with somebody. I'll find out who, too. You're not special."

Lee slurps down the rest of the water and Connor fills it back up and brings it to him. Lee chews on the straw. "You didn't have to take me in," he says.

"It's nice to know you're not going to run off with my things."

"Fuck you mean," Lee mumbles, giggling, sticking his tongue between the gap in his front teeth.

When Lee turns dopey from the painkillers and falls asleep, Connor sets the water on the floor.

With school out, the center swarms with kids from dawn to dusk. Kickball on the dirt field behind the center, trash lids for bases. Danielle pitches and Connor umps and manages a first aid kit of alcohol swabs and bandages, nursing scraped shins and elbows. Afterward the kids eat snacks, ice cream or peanuts, and take turns running through the sprinkler out back.

The center's air conditioner broke three years ago, so Connor buys Danielle a small fan from Walmart and sets it up on her desk. It breaks and he exchanges it. It breaks again. He exchanges it again. As he crawls out from under the front desk to plug the third one into a power strip, she laughs at him, a soft chitter.

"Funny shit, huh?" he says, careful not to hit his head on the desk.

"Just something pathetic about you. I mean that in the best way. Tell me again about when you threw up at the golf course."

In the following weeks, she tells him about her boyfriend, Charles, whom she's known since she was a girl, who's been sober for four years and three months, and who these days wants to move back in with her. One day she wears a necklace from which a dull diamond ring hangs.

"That's supposed to go on your finger," Connor tells her.

She's chewing bubble gum, holding the back door open for him as he winds the hose up before bringing it inside for the night. "Don't worry about it."

"Poor guy."

"He's made his bed."

"Just going to dangle it there in front of him. You're not too forgiving."

"Some women forgive too much. He was skipping in and out for years, getting into shit. I don't need that."

"He's been good to you recently, though."

"What are you, his probation officer?"

"I know how mean you can be," he says.

"The necklace was a compromise."

"So, what's the plan?"

"My plan is to mind my own business. What's yours?"

He carries the hose in. They shut and lock the door behind them, then walk in silence toward the front desk.

She shuns him for four days. Snippy replies and derisive remarks. Then one rainy afternoon, when the center is slow, she sits next to him in the gym and says, "Charles is moving back in."

"You want him to?"

"If I didn't, he wouldn't."

"Save money on rent."

"Never had a problem paying that."

"I'm glad you're done treating me like I'm the devil," he says.

"At this point I don't think there's any stopping you from doing what you want to."

"So, you're going to be kinder to me now."

"Probably not," she replies, smiling.

"I liked you better when you thought I was leaving soon."

"I liked you better when you were."

She shuns him for two days this time.

His runs stretch to ten miles, across soccer fields abandoned to sunbaked dirt, past the scaffolds of buildings disemboweled by fire. His chest swells. His lungs ache.

He emails Charlotte: *It was nice to meet you. My dad's grateful that you're in his life and so am I. I was wondering if you might be interested in taking a look at my résumé. Please don't tell him I asked for your help. I'm just keeping my options open.*

She replies three hours later with the document, annotated and highlighted, and a note: *Our little secret.*

During Danielle's smoke breaks, he bums one and sits on the front step railing. They discuss how to manage the kids, who passed sixth grade, who didn't, whose dad is violent at home, whose uncle just got out of prison, who is looking for a fight, who needs to be talked to sternly, who coolly. He explains to her why she should vote and quit smoking. She tells him about her church, about Charles' mom, Gloria, who helped look after her even when Charles was out of the picture; who babysits EJ and Marquees on a whim without asking Danielle's sister, Erin, for a dime; who takes the boys to White Sox games and always sends them home full, clean, and happy.

She tells stories about Charles.

"He comes in one night—"

"You don't really have girlfriends, do you?" he interrupts.

"I'm making *you* my girlfriend; there's not a soul in the city you can tell anything to. So, he comes in one night. I was at Erin's. EJ was just a baby then. He's in his crib and I'm asleep on the couch next to him. The light by the apartment door is on for when Charles comes home. I couldn't wait up anymore, fell asleep. At two in the morning, Charles sneaks in. So drunk, he could hardly talk. Hiccups that shook his whole body. And he's wearing this raincoat. I'd never seen it before, so I asked him where he got it. He's all shifty, like normal. But finally he tells me that he traded for it. That's when I notice that he doesn't have a shirt on underneath. He's not wearing shoes, either. I said, 'What's going on? Why is your mouth bleeding?' He's like, 'It's not. No, it's cool, baby. It's nothing. I love you, girl.' He'd always say that when he'd done something stupid. 'I love you, baby girl.' I asked him what happened to his shoes and he looks down and realizes that he's not wearing any. 'Nothing, baby girl, it's cool. One and only.'"

Laughing, Danielle pitches her cigarette and lies down on the steps with her hands behind her head.

"So, this is what happened. He got drunk, fell over, and smashed his face. He had blood all over his shirt and didn't want me to find out about it. So…"

She convulses from laughter, hands on her belly. Connor hops down from the railing and leans against it.

"His shirt had blood on it, so he traded it and his shoes to a beggar for the guy's raincoat. Nasty, disgusting coat. Full of holes. Swear to God, the pockets were stuffed with used napkins from every fast-food place in Chicago."

"You love ragging on him."

"Helps me clear my thoughts."

"You know, I went a long time in life before finding any girls funny."

"Maybe you finally met a woman."

Twelve-mile runs. Burst blisters wrapped in athletic tape. Socks stained black with blots of blood. The ice bound to his knees and ankles with old shoelaces melts as he sleeps. When he wakes, he pours the bags out in the sink and checks on Lee.

One afternoon he walks in to find Lee sitting up in bed, facing the window. "What are you doing?" Connor asks.

Lee looks over his shoulder. His pupils are gone. The bags under his eyes are pudgy and purple. He opens his mouth as if about to yell, but he doesn't make a sound. He clicks his jaw, turns back to the window.

Connor stays in the doorway. "Lee."

"No different than all your running around the city."

"Quite a bit, actually."

"All out of pills, too."

"No, you're not."

"They're gone. Traded them in, fuck you mean."

"What do you want me to do with you, huh? I'm calling the cops. Don't go anywhere."

Lee turns and swings his legs up on the bed. "Real fucking funny."

"Lee, I can't do this shit."

"No, I'm done, you see. This is the end for me. I don't have money to buy anything else anyway. And you don't really have shit-else I can pawn but your computer, and I'm too nice to take that. After I'm all clean, I'm going to finish my diploma and go to college and be an astronaut like I always wanted to be."

"I'm adding a bolt to the door."

"Good thinking."

"What will you do for the pain?" Connor asks.

"Pain? I haven't had a moment of pain in my whole life."

"You're taking advantage of me. It's not right."

"Grow up. You know what you're doing. You're not special."

"What if I throw you out?"

"I'll live. Always have. And you're too good for all that type of talk. Shame on you. You love it here. You love the drama. You love your old friend Lee, fuck you mean. Wouldn't even know what to do without me. You haven't learned shit. That's why you're still here. Haven't learned mud from a full diaper."

Lee closes his eyes and starts humming to himself.

Connor hides Lee's cellphone in the silverware drawer and buys an extra bolt for the door. For three weeks, Lee yowls from pain and withdrawals, but he obediently wears his casts and even says please and thank you when Connor tends to him.

Charlotte emails Connor a spreadsheet of job openings: *medical researcher in St. Louis, private school teacher in Kansas City, secretarial assistant to a housing nonprofit in Chicago. Just some opportunities to consider, since you're working on your résumé. Because I travel so much, I have connections all over the Midwest. I'd be happy to set you up with an informational interview somewhere, if you're curious about my line of work. Perhaps we can narrow your search. P.S. How are things going with that girl? Is she starting to like you? I swear, Vanessa got ahold of your dad's daily planner. He's now run into her at the grocery store, the dry cleaners, and the movies. He thinks it's all coincidence. I don't. Of course, the last time we saw her she was with a guy. He seemed like a college bro. He wore a baseball cap with a flat brim and went by Chaz or something. Don't be surprised if your dad brings it up. I've been there myself. She must've really liked you. Best, Charlotte.*

He types: *Thank you for the info and for putting time into this. No, she doesn't like me any more than she did before, but she can stand more of me now than she used to. The more time I spend with her, the more it hurts to be around her, and the more it hurts, the more I want to see her.*

He deletes the last sentence before replying.

On his day off, he puts on an extra pair of socks and runs twenty miles. The muggy, overcast afternoon swathes him in the city's luscious viscera: barbeque food trucks, diesel exhaust, marijuana, restaurant dumpsters. Midway, it drizzles. Toward the end he becomes feverish, gets the chills. After stretching on the landing, he stumbles into his apartment. In the shower, he covers the drain with his feet, and pink water pools beneath his newly broken blisters, hypnotizing him. The lather burns. He eats two hamburgers and falls asleep.

Weeks pass in bouts of heat and sweat and aches and scabs. He buys a hair trimmer to more easily buzz his head.

"So, it was the Fourth of July," Danielle says, pushing a wooden wheeled crate around the gym as Connor walks alongside collecting red and blue plastic dodgeballs and dropping them in the crate. Her hair is braided. She wears black gym shorts and a pink sports bra beneath a white shirt. "Charles was out late and I figured he'd be gone for the night. I went to bed. Then I got a text from a girlfriend that he'd been in an argument with this bar owner. He'd been mouthing off, got thrown out. Whatever. But there was a girl with him who was seeing this other guy named Damion. Damion had been looking for Charles. I just knew something was about to happen. I knew it. I was so worried. In the middle of the night, I walked to Gloria's and borrowed her car to go look for Charles. It was so hot out, oh my God. I couldn't find him and couldn't find him. Suddenly, there he was, crouched beneath this streetlight, all alone. He wasn't asleep, but he had his head resting up against the poll like he was trying to. I pulled up beside him, got him into the car. Meanwhile he was talking about how he wanted to mess Damion up. All that. I called Gloria to let her know I found him. I was tired; it was hot. So I got Charles into the house. I was helping him undress for bed when I saw this piece in his waistband. He'd never been a gun person. I'd never even heard him talk about them. And it was like he forgot he had it, because he didn't say anything about it till he saw the way I was looking at him. When he remembered it, it was like, for a second, I saw something in his face, a little flash of something, his eyes squinting. I didn't like that shit one bit."

"What do you mean?"

"I don't know. He wasn't himself. And if EJ and Marquees had been there, I don't know what I'd have done."

"You think he would do something to you or the boys?"

"No."

"But he could have, you think?"

"No."

Arms full of dodgeballs, Connor stops. Danielle keeps pushing the crate. "Now he's back in the house."

She yawns. "You don't know him. It's not like that. He's harmless. And he's got his shit together better now. Hurry up. I need to get home."

"What if it happens again?"

She stops and turns to face him, one hand on the crate, the other on her hip. She raises her eyebrows and turns her ear to him, as if she didn't hear him.

"Why are you telling me about him?" he asks.

"Just talk. You bothered?"

"If you're not safe."

"Drop this hero shit, would you? I don't need that."

"Just don't want you to be in danger."

"That's exactly what you want. Men either want to hurt you or protect you from it. They don't know anything else," she says. She pushes the crate again. "Whatever. I told you this wouldn't be like that. I told you and you didn't listen. Men never listen. Hurry up, please."

His tone is mild, earnest. "I am really sorry for whatever happened to you to make you so...bitter and angry."

She stops again but doesn't look back at him. "Nothing happened to me. I'm not damaged. You just don't know what life is really like. That's your problem. You don't understand anything. You can't, no matter how much you try. You stumbled in here one day and convinced yourself that if you stumbled in here enough, maybe you and I could start fucking. Maybe we could fall in love and maybe you could take me back to where you came from. But none of that is going to happen."

He walks beside her again, tossing balls in the crate. "If you really thought I was just trying to sleep with you, why let me hang around so much?"

"I can clean up the rest."

"Maybe you wanted some company."

She says nothing.

"Maybe you wanted something else."

"You're an asshole," she says.

"It'd be a lot simpler for you if I were."

He leaves the gym.

For a week they don't talk. Then one day he parks his bike in front of the center as usual, and when he leaves, it's gone. She shrugs when he asks about it.

"Right," he says.

"No idea."

"You're a riot."

After another week of silence, she pokes her head into the

propped-open bathroom doorway while he's scrubbing the urinals with a toilet brush. Fingering the ring on her necklace, she pleasantly steers the conversation toward setting him up with a friend of hers from high school.

With his shoulder he wipes sweat from the side of his face. "What?" he says.

"She's cute. I went to school with her. Sweet as pie."

"Does she know where my bike is?"

"Only God knows that. I'll get you her number."

He scrubs. "Can't tell if you're trying to be really nice or really cruel."

"Why not meet her and find out?"

They smile at each other. Then he laughs and shakes his head and begins scrubbing again. "We have to teach these kids not to piss on the floor. Everyday, the same puddles. Never seen anything like it."

"Let me know if you change your mind," she says.

"Sure thing."

"She's got a nice body."

"Ask Charles. He might be interested."

"You got jokes, too, huh."

He scrubs, doesn't look up. She leaves him.

The last of the season's steam infuses the city. His running shirts won't dry on the landing. At work he tucks a washcloth into his waistband so he can dry his face. For weeks, it seems no one but he enters or exits his apartment complex. The center kids, sluggish and ornery, line up for douses from the hose. He gets a black eye and bruised thigh breaking up a scrum that began over the rights to a lemon-lime popsicle. Lee whistles miserable jazz in the middle of the night.

One afternoon Connor returns from his run to find Lee moaning in the shower, in the fetal position. He helps him up, wraps him in a towel, and escorts him back to bed.

"What happened?"

"I slipped. I heard a crack, thought I broke it again."

"Want me to look at it?"

"You're not special."

"Can't be too bad. Maybe you just scared yourself."

"Never."

"You want to go to the hospital?"

"Fuck that."

Soon, Lee heals enough to lurch about the apartment, at first with the aid of a pool stick, then without.

Once, Connor catches him scrounging through the cupboards. "What do you need?" he asks.

"Nothing. Looking for an ornament of mine. Bet you stole it."

"An ornament?"

"Grandma gave it to me."

"Lee, the pills aren't there anymore."

"Where'd they go?"

"When you got too fussy, I crushed them up and put them in your oatmeal."

"You sly prick."

"We're all out now."

Lee leans his head against the fridge and mumbles to himself.

"Look at you, Lee! Soon, you'll be sprinting in and out of all sorts of dives and basements."

"My savior."

"You look good. How do you feel?"

Lee taps his head against the fridge and sways side to side as though to music. Deep in thought, he walks back to his cot, scratching his chin and mouthing some rap lyrics.

That night the temperature drops twenty degrees in two hours, the clouds rupture, and the slit sky gushes with rainfall. Bottles and cans clatter down the street. Clotheslined shirts flit in the darkness like witches. The storm quits by morning, just after Connor returns from work. He wakes to Lee standing over him.

"Going to see my sister."

"In Charlotte or Durham?"

"What's that supposed to mean?"

"Don't do it, Lee. Get yourself straight."

"My straight is crooked to you, and it goes the same backward."

"You can stay as long as you like."

"Eventually they'll find me out and you'll be out on your ass. There's no good ending for me and you here."

"Come back and see me."

"You better not be here when I get back, fuck you mean."

On the way out, Lee places a hand-stitched snowman ornament on the kitchen counter, which Connor staples to the living room drywall. "Son of a bitch," he says, marveling at it.

Two miles into the day's run, on a quiet residential street, he sees a skinny teenager turning big figure-eights on his stolen bike. Connor runs up behind him, then jumps in front and grabs the handlebars. The teen puts his feet down. "The fuck, man."

"This is my bike."

"Fuck that. I bought it."

"From someone who stole it from me."

"My dad gave me this bike."

"You just said you bought it."

"No, I didn't."

"Get off."

Connor grabs the boy by the collar and drags him off the bike, taking punches in the cheek and ear. He pushes the boy down, pedals to the center, and walks the bike to the front desk, where Danielle sits at the computer. EJ and Marquees play tag in the hallway. Sneakers squeak in the gym.

"You're tracking dirt in here," she says to Connor.

"I'm the one who vacuums."

She stands to look at him, notices the bike, then grins. "It's a miracle."

"Praise God."

He holds his hand out to her. The boys stop playing. "How did you find it, Connor?" Marquees shouts.

"I run all over the city. I always keep my eyes peeled. I spotted the little thief popping wheelies, so I took it back."

She pulls the red tape from a desk drawer, throws it to Connor, then puts her elbow on the desk and rests her chin on her hand, covering her grin with a closed fist.

"Did you beat him up?" EJ asks.

"No. I just explained that it was mine and he gave it back," Connor replies, applying a new strip of tape over the frame.

"Better lock it up better this time," Marquees says.

"You're right. You can never trust those little thieves."

Danielle leans back in her chair, elbows on the armrests. He throws the tape back to her and she catches it in her lap.

"By the way, Danielle, I'm going to find out what you're doing on that computer all the time."

"Sure."

"She doesn't even tell us," EJ replies.

"I'll find out. Be good for your aunt, boys."

Biking home he smiles. He carries his bike up his building's external staircase, then leans it against his bedroom wall. After showering, he wraps himself in a towel, sits on the end of his bed, and looks his bike over, his brow already perspiring again. When he lies back, his phone rings. His heart stammers when he sees that Danielle is calling.

Her voice is hurried but steady. "I just found out, so I'm calling to let you know. Keon was shot last night."

He sits up. "What hospital is he at?"

"No, Connor. He's gone."

Hooded, ashen, Connor drifts among the outer reaches of a candle-less vigil in a small park, an apparition of which most of the gathered are unaware. In suit and tie, Keon's heavyset minister preaches and leads prayers and hymns, each summoned gasp, growl, and hum rehearsed in vigils past. Sinking deeper into twilit darkness, the crowd soon senses itself only by its keens and sniffles. When Connor's strained eyes can strain no more, he pinches them shut. He no longer hears the minister, but Keon's sisters and aunts wailing. Keon's friends lie down in patches of dead grass, juddering with grief, whimpering. His girlfriend, nineteen and six months pregnant, wipes her eyes with the belly of her sweatshirt, then presses it hard against her face and frees as many muffled shrieks as her lungs can bear. His friends from the rec center punch their open palms and curse, and his mother storms back and forth across the park, shaking her head. Enfeebled, she stumbles into Connor and buries her damp face in his chest. As she bellows, he enfolds her in his tendrilous arms. Together they weep.

The next day, on the sunny and windless afternoon of the funeral, the center is empty and the cemetery packed. Mauve weed flowers infest the dried grass around Keon's grave, over which his mahogany casket, purchased with a crowdsourced collection of two thousand dollars, hovers, suspended by two blue straps. The solemn closed casket transfixes the congregation. On the other side of the chain-link fence bordering the cemetery, a youth soccer practice ends. The kids wander over, grip the fence with their tiny fingers, and peer through its rhombuses, frowning. Danielle stands in front of Connor, EJ and Marquees on either side of her. She stoically watches the minister talk of the Shepherd's care for His sheep. She seems too angry to blink.

Days later the cops discover Keon's killer with gunshot wounds in his chest, abdomen, and head. Danielle's boss begins closing the center at five o'clock every day, urges the kids to stay out of the streets. Gloria watches EJ and Marquees for Erin. The authorities question six men Connor plays basketball with, arresting and charging two of them with first-degree murder. Stray bullets riddle a garage two blocks from the center, so Danielle bars some of the regulars from playing basketball. When a few refuse to leave, she threatens to call the cops. When they start playing on the outdoor courts, she rolls a jarful of marbles out onto the gravel. Cussing, her nephews disperse.

"They're not safe out there," Connor tells her, sweeping up the marbles.

"Nobody's safe if they're here. Not now, anyway. I should've known better."

"How could you have known any of this would happen?"

She scoffs.

Connor can now hear the difference between firecrackers, backfiring vehicles, and gunshots. He keeps his phone with him, even when he runs, in case Danielle calls. His back and neck tighten from stress. He loses ten pounds, sleeps four hours a day.

One afternoon in the office, Danielle barks at him when he asks when the center will return to its regular hours. "Don't talk to me like that; I don't sleep on your couch," he replies.

"Always with something to say."

They stare at each other for half a minute, then she looks away and replies, "I don't know when we'll go back to the old hours."

He leans against the wall, looks out at the front desk. "Will you bring the boys around soon? I miss them."

"I will. They haven't forgotten you."

"I'm really sorry about Keon."

"How many times did I tell him not to fuck around?"

"Many times," he says.

"How many times did I tell him what could happen?"

"I know you did."

She begins shuffling papers, rummaging in filing cabinets, sharpening pencils. "He wouldn't listen. They never do. They don't think the reality of what they're getting themselves into applies to them. They don't get it till it's too late. Then shit gets out of control, and they come to you for help, and what are you supposed to do?"

"There's nothing you could've done."

"That's not what I'm trying to say. Shut up for a minute and listen to me."

He watches her, scratching his lip with his fingernail.

"It's not like that," she continues. "What I'm saying is that Keon did everything he could to get what he got. I wish he hadn't gotten it, but he did nothing to stop it. He was careless. I can't even feel too bad for him, because I've seen enough of this shit happen to kids who did nothing to deserve it. All my worries go to them. All my fear and sadness and anger. I wish I had more to give them. If I was stronger."

"You're very strong, Danielle."

"Just listen to me." She pulls a stack of pamphlets from the cabinet, taps them on her knee to align their edges, and puts them back. "I'm telling you this because you don't have anybody to rat me out to. I know it makes me sound weak and petty and childish. And callous. But I can't afford to have much sympathy for Keon. Not when I've seen kids half his age who haven't so much as raised their voices in their lives, seen them shot or neglected or had a doctor diagnose them with something terrible. Because there's only so much heart of mine to go around and I can't do anything but be cold and angry that I'm wasting my compassion on this stupid boy who fucked his life up for nothing. And I know you disagree with me, and I know you have a thousand comments you'd like to make, but nothing you have to say would make me feel any different about it. I don't want you to tell me that he had a chance to be a good young man if he turned things around, and that nobody deserves to die, and that life should be fairer for us. I don't need to hear any of that from you. I already know it. Don't tell me how strong and good-hearted I am when I don't feel like I'm either. You understand?"

"Okay."

She closes her eyes, breathes deeply. After a minute, she says, "Okay, what?"

"Okay, I'm not going to say anything."

"Okay."

She closes the cabinet, sits down on the swivel chair, and throws her head back.

"What else?" he asks.

"What do you mean?"

"What else do you need?"

She looks at him. When she holds her hand out, he walks to her and takes it. Her eyes well, but when she blinks, no tears fall down her cheeks. He squeezes her hand, then lets go.

She brings EJ and Marquees into the center the next day. They and a dozen other preschool kids play softball in the gym, Connor pitching underhand. By the time school starts that fall, the center returns to its old hours and Marquees again spends his days with his aunt.

For his attendance and job performance, the warehouse rewards Connor with a quarter-an-hour raise. He buys new socks, trashes the holey, threadbare ones. He buys sweatshirts and a stocking cap for the fall. Soon the strain in his neck recedes. He sleeps deeply again, dreams of fistfights throughout which he's paralyzed by fear, of Minnesota summer picnics with Danielle, Bill, and Charlotte.

As the days grow colder and shorter, Danielle's laughter

sounds different to him, unabated, higher in pitch. She and the kids prank him by hiding his bike behind a rack of basketballs in the gym's storage closet. When Connor grills Marquees, the boy tattles on her.

She tells Connor stories about growing up in foster care with Erin, cooking for ten transient siblings, stirring pots of spaghetti noodles with a fork, having girls she'd come to trust threaten to pull knives on her; about meeting Charles, a skinny high school loudmouth whose voice cracked until he was twenty-two, who concocted fantastic lies, sometimes to shirk responsibilities, sometimes for fun. He claimed relation to many famous rappers, to have disorders and diseases that no one had heard of, to have slept with every sexy girl in Chicago, and to know the whereabouts of long-missing persons. Danielle explains how, finding him harmless and disbelieving him entirely, she never had her guard up.

"It felt good, at times, but that's where I slipped up," she says. "How come we don't check ourselves better when what we're doing feels good?"

She talks about hiding cash from Charles when he came home late. Shoe boxes, false floorboards, broken sink pipes, and couch cushions. "It became this sport," she says. "Then I wanted to make my own money; that way I could keep it from him easier. That's how I came to the center. A little power feels good."

She asks him about Bill and Charlotte, about med school and his friends back home, about his future plans. He swears he has none.

That fall, near the end of his shift, Connor trips while jogging down the warehouse's metal staircase. He twists his ankle and sprains his wrist. He bikes home, ices his swelling joints, then wraps his ankle in electrical tape. He limps for half a mile and jogs for two more before he can begin his run. Chilly winds stiffen his muscles. Cold flickers of sunlight blind him. Before bed, he swaddles his ankle with his belt, and just as he's falling asleep, Bill calls to tell him he and Charlotte are marrying in the spring. "That's wonderful, Dad," Connor groans.

"I'd like you to be my best man."

"I'd be honored."

"Everything okay? You sound sick."

"I'm fine. How come you're getting married?"

"What do you mean?"

"It's a huge decision, Dad."

"It's what people do when they love one another."

"There's nothing wrong with that answer."

"What's the problem, then?"

"There is no problem," Connor replies. "It's great news. It's just…it's a forever thing."

"Of course it's forever. What makes you think I don't know that?"

"Don't get defensive."

"I'm not," Bill says. "You're so young, Connor. And wise, too. But there are things you won't understand till you get older. I'm in a good place. Charlotte's an extraordinary woman."

"What are you trying to say?"

"Nothing. You sure you're okay? It sounds like something's not right."

"Tired."

"Working too much?"

Connor pauses, then says, "I knew shit would be tougher here than if I stayed home. I just didn't know how. Now it's starting to sink in."

"Yeah?"

"But don't worry about me. Everything's fine. Actually just twisted my ankle."

"Take time off work. I'll send you money."

"Stop, Dad."

They're silent for a minute.

"Just be happy for me, then. For us," Bill says.

"I am."

"Good."

"I didn't mean anything," Connor says.

"I know you didn't."

"Can I still be your best man?"

"You might need to fight James for it."

"Don't give me a reason."

The next day Danielle shadows Connor as he dust mops the gym. The kids stand in the gym entrance, shoving one another. "Hurry up, Connor!" one of them yells.

"We'll get on without you for a few days," she says. "You should rest." He crosses back and forth across the tiles, collecting a growing strip of dirt and hair and dust. He doesn't reply. "I see. You're too tough, can't help yourself. At least use some of the supplies in the first aid kit if you need to."

"A while back, I asked Charlotte to look at my résumé," he says suddenly. "She and my dad would help me set myself up with something else. Anywhere, really."

"Anywhere?" She crosses her arms, looks down at her shoes. "I've given up trying to talk sense into you, but…like, what the fuck is your deal?" she whispers.

"Did I tell you my dad's getting married?"

"You hear me?" He hides from her eyes. "You are some type of stubborn," she says.

"Charlotte's awesome, but I think part of it is that he's afraid of growing old alone."

"Maybe he's just getting on with his life. People do that sometimes, you know."

"When are *you* getting married?"

"This has nothing to do with me."

When she crosses midcourt, the kids start playing basketball on the hoop behind her.

She says, "Why tell me you could be anywhere else if you didn't want me to tell you to go?"

He passes back and forth.

"I won't apologize for looking out for you," she continues.

"I don't know why I told you. Just trying to be honest."

"So, what are you going to do?"

"About what?"

He sweeps the filth into a pile in the corner of the gym, shakes off the mop, rests his chin on the end of the wooden handle, and watches the kids' game. She stands next to him and turns to watch, too.

He says, "Marriage might be good for him, for all I know. It'll help with his income tax. I don't want him to grow old alone, either. Definitely not if he's afraid to."

"Why didn't things work out between him and your mom?"

"She left us."

"That's terrible."

"I love my dad. But drive someone to it, you'll see how terrible they can be."

"You blame him?"

"He has this way of acting like there's nothing more to life than comfort. And it wouldn't be so sad to see if he himself didn't want more that."

"You should trust him to make his own decisions."

"I *should*."

"You're arrogant."

"Yes," he says. "Anyway, I like it here. If I didn't, I'd leave."

"But you asked Charlotte to look at your résumé."

"I'm happy."

"Rest your ankle, stupid."

"It's fine."

"Anyway, the bathroom toilet is backed up again. Wish I'd noticed it sooner. It's a mess now."

"Yes, ma'am."

As he sweeps the filth into a dustpan, she walks out of the gym, stopping on the way to block EJ's jump shot from behind. Delighted, the kids whoop and yelp.

On the day of winter's first snowfall, his landlord knocks on his door. When he opens it for her, she steps just inside the apartment, texting. She wears a baby blue, knee-length dress. Ointment covers a new tattoo on her bare right shoulder, an angel. She puts her phone away and, turning her head to finger one of half a dozen earrings, she tells him that Lee overdosed. "He'd been dead for a while before they found him."

"Where is he?"

"Cook County takes them. Not sure where to. I think they're cremated."

"Did someone tell his wife?"

"They'd been divorced a long time."

"What about his son?"

"No idea. I can take your rent check now. Save you the trip to my office."

"I'll bring it later."

"Sorry. I know you two were friends."

Her phone buzzes. She glares at the text and walks away muttering.

Over the following week, winter chokes the city out. Gaunt boulevards of frozen morning dew. Icy streets and horizontal sleet. Beggars flood the clinic lobbies and shelters and fast food haunts. Connor wears gloves, a hat, and three sweatshirts when he runs. His breaths spill forth in violent blooms. His teeth ache. His knuckles split open.

Danielle tells him she and Erin are in a jam, asks if he can watch the boys. She drops them off at the warehouse early in the morning, and Connor looks after them. Marquees sleeps in the breakroom. Connor pays EJ twenty dollars to help mop the warehouse and prepare orders. Then they walk to his apartment, Connor carrying Marquees. They eat cereal and play cards. When Danielle comes for the boys, she goes no farther than the doorway. Marquees takes his time tying his shoes.

"Is that the gift?" she asks, pointing at the snowman.

"You like it?"

She smiles. "It smells in here."

"There's no one to freshen up for. You can look around if you want to, or you can stand there like the pizza guy."

She looks at him. "Hurry up, boys."

"Everything okay?"

"Thanks for the help. Really, it's easiest when you're available. Fewer eyes, fewer questions."

"Let me do it again sometime. With a little warning, I could plan something fun. Zoo or a baseball game, even."

"Marquees, those shoes aren't going to tie themselves."

The heater in his apartment quits. His landlord won't answer the phone. He wears his stocking cap to bed, sleeps cocooned in quilts, and wakes with the chills, a sore throat, and a stuffed nose. Fifteen degrees warmer than his apartment, the warehouse is a welcomed refuge. He returns to his apartment to find that the heater has, miraculously, turned back on.

Danielle calls him on his night off and asks if he can watch the boys for the night. "Of course. I'll come pick them up."

"No, I'll drop them off."

"I can take the bus, save you the trouble."

"I have Gloria's car. They've eaten and cleaned up. We're already on the way."

"What if I'd said no?"

She laughs. "Right."

He meets them in front of his building. The boys wear their school backpacks. As soon as he steps inside the apartment, EJ pulls out some DVDs and asks where Connor's laptop is.

"Your aunt said you have to do your homework first," Connor reminds him.

"I lost it."

"Are you sure?"

"It's gone."

"She said that if you don't do it, you have to leave your DVDs here."

"No, she didn't."

"Want to find out?"

EJ completes his math and English worksheets, then picks out a movie. They make popcorn. After the boys brush their teeth and curl up on the couch for bed, Marquees asks him, "Where did Keon go to?"

"Heaven."

"That's what Auntie says."

"Always listen to her. She's smart."

"Kids at school say he's in hell," EJ says.

"They're wrong."

"How do you know, Connor?"

"If your aunt says so, it has to be true."

In the morning, he walks EJ to his usual bus stop, sees him onto the bus, then calls Danielle. "I packed him a lunch, too. A bologna sandwich and pudding and celery."

"You didn't have to do all that. He gets lunch at school."

"I'm going to show Marquees where the Bulls play, then we'll see you at work."

"Careful with my baby."

The day is bright and arctic. Marquees holds Connor's hand when they cross streets. They bus to the United Center, stand in the parking lot. Connor points at the giant Bulls posters on the side of the building.

"What's that?" Marquees asks.

"That's where the team plays."

"No, they don't."

"Yes, they do."

"Doesn't look like it."

"The court's inside," Connor explains.

"Really? Can we see it?"

"Maybe someday."

Before they go, Connor shows him the statue of Michael Jordan.

"Who's that?"

"You know who that is."

"No."

"It's MJ."

"Oh. Where's LeBron's statue?"

"Doesn't have one."

"He's better than Jordan."

"You sound crazy."

Marquees giggles.

"You getting cold?" Connor asks.

Marquees nods. On the bus ride home he asks, "Jordan's better than you?"

"Definitely."

"He's not better than my uncle."

"Yeah?"

"No way."

"Jordan was really good."

"Uncle Charles is good."

"Yeah?"

"Could you beat him?"

"Charles?"

"Yeah."

Connor pauses. "I don't know."

❧

Connor Skypes with Charlotte, who calls him from the corner booth of a busy downtown Minneapolis coffee shop, wearing a charcoal blazer and eggshell blouse, her curled hair tucked behind her ears. He answers from a stool in his kitchen.

"Actually, I asked him."

"Why?"

"I'm not the type of woman to wait around for men to figure it out."

"No. I mean, why do you want to marry him?"

She clears her throat, sips her coffee. "Why wouldn't I?"

"I asked him the same question, why he wants to marry you."

"What did he say?"

"He said he loves you."

"And I love him," she replies cheerily.

"I'm surprised. I always thought he'd be an old bachelor."

"You often seem skeptical of his judgment."

"I'm skeptical of everyone. It's not personal."

"I think it's very personal," she says. "You have high standards for him."

He blows his cheeks out, shrugs, and sighs. "Somewhere beneath all his wanting to be one of the boys is a courageous and deeply moral person. Sometimes I get tired of wishing he'd come out more."

"But I see that man all the time."

"You're lucky, then. He'll be a good husband."

"And you'll be a good stepson."

"Hadn't thought about that. By the way, thank you for helping with my job search. I looked at what you sent me."

"And?"

"Honestly, I haven't considered anything too seriously. It was just something to think about."

"You're going to stay?"

"I don't know."

"How are things with Danielle? You still haven't told your dad about her."

"He wouldn't have anything helpful to say. He plays everything safe."

"Don't you?"

He runs his hands over his cropped hair. "I try to see things from her perspective. Suppose it worked out, what would that even look like? I can't shake the feeling that I screwed up, like, I'm too late for something I never had a fair chance to make on time in the first place."

"You didn't sound so defeated the last time we talked."

"I'm getting a clearer picture of what will happen here."

"And you're scared," she says.

"Yes."

"But that's why you left, no? At least in part?"

"To be scared?"

"To find something that scares you."

One morning he exits the warehouse side door and finds a man parked in a white mid-90s Cavalier, rusted and battered, smoke slinking from its cracked window. Connor walks his bike to the driver's side door. His shoulders are tense, but he keeps his fists from balling. The man rolls down the window, wearing an oil-stained taupe mechanics polo, his name printed on the left breast. His eyes are clear but tired. He nods at Connor, and Connor nods back. Then he unlocks the door. Connor puts his bike in the trunk and gets in.

"Lift home?" Charles says.

"Thanks."

In silence, Charles starts driving. At length, he says, "I appreciate you looking after my nephews."

"No problem."

"She says you and her are friends."

"We're at the center together a lot. You know where to go?"

The man nods. "We're engaged, you know."

"Congratulations."

He flicks his cigarette, lights another, and offers Connor one. Connor shakes his head. "I forgot, you're a runner."

"Here and there."

At a stoplight, Charles scratches his left shin with the sludge-caked bottom of his right boot. He doesn't look over. When he hits the gas, he takes the wheel with his right hand and talks into his shoulder. His voice deepens. "My mom means the world to her. To both of us, I mean, but Danielle doesn't always say thanks for what people do. She doesn't like to say things sometimes. But we need to be with my mom now. You wouldn't believe all that goes in to being sick. Then Danielle says something to me about you the other day. Got me thinking, since we're engaged. Maybe you hadn't heard it, I thought. So I should tell you myself. Like I said, Danielle doesn't always say things."

"She's got a ring hanging from her neck."

Charles' laugh is a series of chuckles, as if he's trying to be discrete about hacking up what's caught in his throat. "That's her way."

He drops Connor off at his apartment complex. Connor takes his bike out of the trunk, walks to the driver's window, and thanks him for the ride.

Charles says, "Do me a favor. Don't tell her we talked."

"Okay."

"Thanks again about the boys. You ever need something in return, let us know," Charles adds, lighting another cigarette as he drives off.

It takes Connor the rest of the day to realize that what he

doesn't like about Charles is that he can find little to not like about him.

❧

Connor calls home at Christmas, learns all about Charlotte's sister and brother-in-law in Minnesota. Bill tries to set him up with his coworker's daughter. "She's so smart, Connor. And pretty. If things work out, she could be your date to the wedding."

"I'm real busy, Dad."

Midwinter is long and crisp and dry. Connor's running clothes chafe him. At night, his nose bleeds; the droplets spatter onto his yellowed sheets. Danielle wears jeans, black boots, earmuffs, and colorful sweaters. More and more, her winter-blanched cheeks are eager to lift into smiles. More and more, she glances at him with affection, lust, and anger. She wants to listen to him, to be heard by him. She wants him to leave. She wants to never see him again. She wants to argue with him, to hurt him. She wants to touch him. She wants to kiss him. When they're alone out in front of the center, she occasionally asks him sudden, peculiar questions, post-drag, as though asking requires the spurs of nicotine hits. Does he ever pray? Who's his favorite athlete? Will he marry someday? Does he like Cajun food? Has he ever been with a prostitute?

"A what? What kind of question is that?"

"That's not an answer."

She sits on a frigid metal folding chair by the door, facing him, her legs crossed and hood up, smoking. He sits across from her in his stocking cap, his hands in his jacket pockets and his chair angled toward the street. Another early dusk.

"It's what you're going to get," he replies.

"I'll assume the answer is yes, then."

He stands, hunches against the breeze. "You've gotten away with a lot of shit in your life, haven't you?"

"I get away with whatever I can, like everyone else."

"You and Charles still make love?"

"That's personal."

"Right."

"Anyway, we have sex."

"Good. That's what we're all here for."

"We're here to give a damn about one another. You know that already, otherwise you wouldn't be here with these kids. What you need is the Holy Spirit. You should come to my church."

"Thanks."

"What, you have something better to do?"

"I haven't been to church in many years."

"Doesn't matter. Come with me and Gloria. You can sit with us or in the back by yourself, and you can leave whenever you want."

"What's in it for me?"

"Salvation."

"Of course."

"What's it like to be an atheist and think there's nothing out there for us? Like, how do you get through all the sad times?"

"When's the last time you had sex?" She leans back in her chair, uncrosses her legs. "Too far?" he asks. "Funny how you can ask about my faith, which, if it means anything to me, is a really delicate subject, but I can't ask you—"

"Last night."

"You lie."

"Not long ago, I promise."

"Who said I was an atheist?" he asks.

"You act like one."

"No, no. There has to be something out there for us, otherwise there'd be no purpose to all the suffering. Not that I've known hardship, really." His hands still in his pockets, he bounces up and down on the balls of his feet to warm himself. "You still enjoy it?"

"It's sex."

"I didn't ask whether it was sex."

She flicks her cigarette butt into the ice cream pail by the door and puts her icy hands on her cheeks. "You should follow through with medical school. You'd be a great doctor. A pediatrician. Or else you could do humanitarian work somewhere. There's so much good you could bring to needy people."

"I'm done with medicine."

"How about a lawyer, then? There aren't enough good ones, like the type looking out for those who need it most. If you want to help kids, you should get in the trenches. These prosecutors fuck a lot of lives up even before the judges get involved. Damn, it's cold out here."

"Let's go inside."

She hugs herself, looking out at the darkening street. "There was a time," she says, "when I liked pleasuring him more than I liked being pleasured. I used to enjoy feeling like I was in control. I was young. When you're powerless, there's only so much you can do to gain it over somebody else."

"You look cold. Let's head in."

"Okay."

"You want my hat?"

She sniffles. "No, thanks. I used to like it best when he hadn't showered since coming home from work and there was that stink to him, sweat and dirt and oil, that stuck to his clothes and his skin...I can't really explain it. And after, that was my favorite time, wrapped up in it. But that seems like a long time ago. I sound old, much older than I am. Whatever. All that I used to care about doesn't matter anymore. Now I'm saying too much. It's cold out."

"You going to marry him?"

"Hasn't crossed my mind in a while, to be honest."

"Is it poetry?" he asks.

"Is *what* poetry?"

"Is that what you're always doing on the computer?"

She looks up at him, smiles tenderly, and shakes her head, then she looks back toward the street. "It's Gloria. She has cancer. There are so many appointments and doctors and specialists and bills. I try to read up on everything I can. I try to take notes and arrange things for her."

"What type?"

"Started in her kidneys, then spread to her lungs."

He blows air into his hands. "That's awful."

Lighting another cigarette, she stands and turns to watch a passing car. "Go in without me."

"You want my coat?"

"No."

"Danielle, I'm so sorry about Gloria."

She looks back over her shoulder and studies his face. In the remaining daylight, he can just make out her dry eyes. Wanting to kiss her, he backs toward the door and leans against it. She turns to face him and stares at her boots while she talks, drawing curlicues with her cigarette.

"I've decided I can't be any sadder about it than she is, and she's at peace. Setting aside all the pain. Spiritually, I mean. She says she's had a lifetime of prayer to prepare her for this. That's a beautiful thing. But…" She pauses to suck deeply and exhale through her nose. "If you're going to stand out here and shiver, then I might as well tell you what I think about all your…" She closes her eyes when the word she's searching for escapes her.

"Charm?"

"No."

"Charisma?"

"No, no, no. Give me a second."

"Swagger?"

"Ignorance, actually," she replies, opening her eyes again, looking at him. "*Ignorance* is the word; my brain's frozen. You do too much thinking and too much worrying, and it makes you stupid. Just my opinion. Like, I know what's different about you and why you'll never blend in here. Because most people I know can't afford to fret things like you do. I don't think you realize the luxuries you have. Doubting and questioning and considering everything, those are things most people can't afford. I worry about you."

"You do?"

She finishes her cigarette, walks it to the pail, and leans her shoulder against the door, a few feet from him. "Because you could overthink things till what's most wonderful in life, the shit that matters a hell of a lot to most everybody, doesn't matter to you. Maybe it's true that everything we do is dumb and we do it for no good reason, but that doesn't mean it's not important. You don't need reasons to do good works, and you already know that, of course. But I worry you'll pretend you don't know it or you'll forget it. Just my opinion. I might be wrong."

She looks up at him innocently, wary, for the first time, of offending him.

"But I have more reasons to be here than I ever had to stay back home."

"Yeah?" she says.

"Yeah."

"I don't know." She watches a group of boys walk along the sidewalk across the street. When they're out of sight, she repeats, "I don't know."

She goes inside, and after five minutes of shivering and thinking, he follows.

❧

As the days lengthen, he sheds layers and takes longer

runs, slopping through slushy puddles, trotting atop sheets of ice, striding over unforgiving cement that stabs his knees with jolts of pain throughout miles one, six, and twelve, like clockwork. Ice and aspirin and heat and shots of liquor. Using a flathead screwdriver, he scrapes chewing gum from the worn-smooth soles of his shoes. A quarter of the way through a twenty-mile route, he stops and vomits in a McDonald's toilet for fifteen minutes. He drinks a cup of water, buys fries, eats a few, and gives the rest to a man holding a "homeless veteran" sign. He finishes his run. Back home, he catches sight of his naked body in the bathroom mirror, his sinew-draped bones, and pauses to fill his lungs. On his nights off, he turns on the flashing red blinker attached to his handlebars and cruises through quiet neighborhoods, snaking down empty streets, admiring the stars.

Leaving work on Easter morning, he places his foot on his pedal and glances up to see a man and his son standing side by side fifteen yards in front of him. The man is neckless and meaty, hands nonchalantly folded mid-chest, rings on his fingers. He looks at Connor. When the teen points at the bike and starts cussing, Connor recognizes him. "Fuck," Connor says.

"Don't ride off," the man says. "I'll just come back tomorrow. Leave the bike and that'll be that." The man wears black sweatpants and a gray long-sleeved shirt that stretches over his belly. "Come on. My boy's friends all saw you take it. How could a grown man pull a knife on a kid, and over a bike at that?"

Connor looks at him, then at the teen. He swallows and steps off his bike and holds it against his hip. "I have the receipt for this at my apartment."

"Me too," the kid replies.

"I'll meet you there and show it to you."

"I got shit to do today," the man replies.

"So do I," Connor says.

When they start toward him, he looks down at the bike, groans, sticks his leg through the frame, and looks up at them again. Just steps away, they freeze. The father frowns and the son's eyes widen in astonishment. Connor falls onto his back, pulling the bike on top of him. He hugs the frame and locks his hands together and kinks his foot through the front wheel's spokes. He waits, watching the pair through the back wheel pressed against his face.

His brow already speckled with sweat, the man rubs his lips with his fingers. "Fuck this," he says as he takes off his shirt and hands it to his son. His pecs are mountainous slabs, his gut a planet. He pulls his sagging sweats up over his butt. "Got shit to do today."

Connor closes his eyes and tightens his limbs, like so much chain, about his bike. The man grabs the front wheel, drags him across the lot, and thrashes him side to side. Connor's shirt tears open and the gravel shreds his back. His clammy hands slip off the frame. He grabs it again. Panting, the man kneels on the bike, crushing him. When Connor opens his eyes and glares up at him, the man starts punching. He misses Connor once, striking the ground, then connects again and again. He pounds Connor's shoulder and ribs and face. Connor chips a molar on the ground, blacks out, then regains consciousness to discover his body still clinging to his bike.

The man peels Connor's hands from the frame and jerks the bike away, but Connor's legs stay latched. He rolls on top of the bike and stares at the gravel, grimacing as the man kicks him in the kidneys and thighs.

Then, as abruptly as the punches began, they stop. Connor wheezes, bracing himself for more, but after thirty seconds of silence, he turns on his side and pushes himself away from the man with his free foot, dragging his bike with him. He opens wide the eye that isn't swollen shut. The man sits, watching sweat stream down his chest and over his belly, heaving for air. The teen stands off to the side with his hands on his head and his mouth hanging open, his father's shirt slung over his shoulder.

"Shit," the man says between breaths. He rolls to one side and places his clenched fist on the ground to steady himself as he stands. He takes his shirt from his son, dries his face and neck. "This is your bike, huh?" he says to Connor.

Connor glares at the teen, who avoids his father's gaze.

"Fuck, boy. We got shit to do today, don't we?"

The son says nothing as his father grabs him by the back of the neck and leads him away. Connor closes his eye and listens to his breaths. When he opens it again, he's alone.

Danielle texts Connor after two days of his no-shows: *coming in?*

He texts: *no im dead*

He sleeps on his back, his hands on his chest, a bottle of whiskey on the floor by the bed. The left side of his face is swollen and plum purple. His eyelid droops over his eye. He wakes when Danielle sits on the end of his bed. She wears jeans and a white tank top. Her ring necklace is gone. She looks him over, then examines the bike on the floor beside him. The wheels are bent, the chain twisted, the frame scratched. She lifts his shirt. Lime and blackberry and ruby bruises parade along his obliques like a rash. He falls asleep.

She wakes him again with a plate of baked chicken breast and steamed broccoli.

"Where'd you get the food?" he asks.

"Grocery store. I did the dishes for you, too. After we eat, let's go to the doctor."

"Nothing's broken. Just bruises. What's a doctor going to

do about bruises, tell me to wait? I only need a new tooth." He pulls his cheek aside with his finger and shows her the broken tooth. The blood between his teeth is coal black.

"Should I be impressed by that?"

"No."

"Stop winking."

"Don't make me laugh—it hurts."

"How will you work?"

"I told my boss I got jumped, so he's giving me a few days off. Even let me use my sick pay. Nice of him."

"How will you get there? The wheels are all fucked up now, anyway."

"I have money for a new one," he says.

"Back home?"

"Saved up. If I ask my dad for money, I'll have to tell him why I need it. He'd have the National Guard here in a day."

"But you're going home for the wedding in a month."

"I know."

He sits up to eat. He tells her what happened.

"That might be the dumbest story I've ever heard."

"What's so dumb about it?"

"You."

"You think I should've just given it to him?"

"Obviously. Then again, what you did makes about as much sense as anything else you've done since I met you."

She washes his dishes and retrieves Lee's painkillers from the back of the freezer, where Connor hid them last summer. He takes two pills and she talks with him until they kick in.

"There's beer," he whispers goofily, beginning to fall asleep. "There's coffee, tea..."

"I'm fine. Just rest."

"Thank you so, so, so much for all your...you know, you do so much."

"You're welcome. I'll come check on you tomorrow."

He smiles at her.

"You're high."

"Yeah."

She looks at her nails and says, "Kicked Charles out again."

"Really?"

"Just one bottle is all I found. But he was getting mouthy, too. I suppose I'll let him come back at some point."

"Carol has a cot I can use."

"You won't be tough enough on him."

"No. No, probably not."

"Now he calls and texts every day telling me that he did nothing wrong and that I misunderstood things."

"You're cruel."

"Yep."

"But you're an aunt… Sorry. I meant to say that you're a *great aunt*." He closes his eye and whispers inaudibly. Then he says, "You're so incredible to me that…it's just fucking painful to know you."

She bites her inner lip and touches his stomach. "You're high," she says.

"Yeah. Pretty fucked up."

"You should sleep."

"Marquees doesn't know who Michael Jordan is."

"Michael *who*?"

He looks at her.

"Just kidding."

He closes his eye again. "I'll take him and EJ to a game next winter."

"That's not cheap."

"I'll save up."

Soon he falls asleep.

The next day she cleans his living room and takes his sheets and clothes to the laundromat. He showers, shaves, and brushes his teeth. His urine is pink. For lunch she fixes them plates of tuna salad and potato chips. She sits on a stool next to his bed, staring out the window as she chews. After washing his dishes and wiping down his kitchen and folding his clothes, she gives him the remaining pills.

When she comes the next day, he's standing in the kitchen drinking coffee. They take the bus downtown and he buys another used bike. He goes back to work the following day, crouching and shuffling, his sclera scarlet, the bag under his eye as dark as grapes, his bruises butterscotch blotches. He leaves his old bike on the landing, and when he comes home from work the next morning, it's gone.

The rec center kids gawk at him when he returns.

"Got his ass beat!" one boy yells.

"Just fell down the stairs," he says.

"Never seen a staircase that long," a girl replies.

He scowls at the girl and the kids go quiet. When his lips break upward into a smirk, the kids bust into laughter.

Spring rouses the green of scraggly ash and maple trees, of balconied flower garden troughs. Unable to run, he walks, trying to see the city anew: the inflatable swimming pools awaiting summer; the bus driver who eats a package of licorice every day; the men smoking on their unpainted porches; the kids shooting hoops on the netless rims of fenced-in courts. Her nephews.

"Why are you doing that, Connor?" EJ asks him.

"What do you mean?"

"You're looking at me funny."

"Sorry. It's nothing, buddy."

"Auntie says you might be crazy."

"Might be," Connor replies.

"She's crazy, too."

"Might be."

❧

Two weeks later he flies home. On a quiet suburban Saturday afternoon—in a small Catholic church with flower gardens contouring the serpentine sidewalk that leads to the cement front steps, and a stained-glass crucifix façade between two fawn brick towers—Bill and Charlotte stand beneath a rose-threaded wicker arbor and exchange vows before their friends and family. Connor stands beside his father. Charlotte's sister, Lisa, stands beside her. Afterward, the congregants proceed to the secluded back room of a downtown Minneapolis restaurant. Crisply folded napkins, polished silverware, and servers as dapper as their guests await them. Tediously ironed white tablecloths cover five round tables of ten, four encircling the master's in the middle, over which a crystal chandelier hangs from the vaulted ceiling. Next to the tiered wedding cake in a corner of the room, a quartet—a cellist, two violinists, and a classical guitarist—play classical hits and R&B.

Connor's hair is coifed neatly to one side, his face shaven, his eyes sober and elusive. Though the swelling in his cheeks has subsided, Lisa, a lilac corsage on her wrist, spent thirty minutes of her morning applying makeup to the discolored bruises on his face.

Vanessa, conspicuously seated behind him, wears a short pink dress and a pearl necklace. Her newly cut hair reaches just below her chin. Her date, Dean, is a garrulous blond with thick-rimmed glasses, wearing a navy blue overcoat, a saffron bowtie, and a white dress shirt with black buttons. From time to time, his hyenic cackling fills the room. She doesn't acknowledge Connor, and he avoids looking her way. Instead, he focuses on the Old Fashioneds James forces on him and, as those at the head table chat, on the fork with which he corrals rogue cherry tomatoes glazed with ranch dressing, disentangles raw onions from his lettuce, and clusters them on the edge of his plate.

Knowing that Vanessa's invitation was Bill's doing, Connor glances at Charlotte, who spares an instant from her conversation with Lisa to roll her sympathetic eyes at him as she cups the bouquet of stunning curls behind her head. It's a tic she adopts for the night, as if ensuring that all is in its right place on her wedding day. Connor shakes his head.

The newlyweds cut their cake, and a photographer and videographer document them as they hand-feed each other small slices. The room laughs and swoons.

Whenever the slivered ice cubes in his drink clink together, Connor tips the glass back and chews them down, then orders another. Amid several hours of dancing, singing, and drinking, he catches up with relatives and introduces himself to Charlotte's family, occasionally stepping outside to chain-smoke beneath an entryway redwood pergola with vine-covered posts and lightbulbs strung along the joists.

A fellow smoker, Dean strikes up a conversation with him, and they soon abandon their overcoats as Dean talks about his and Vanessa's social work program, his undone bowtie hanging from his neck. As he talks, he anxiously swoops his thick bangs upward with his right hand. Connor taps his dress shoes against the bricks lining the pavement.

"Social justice, man. That's where it's at," Dean says.Connor nods. "Know what I'm saying?"

"No."

Dean tugs on his bangs. "Every level, national down to city council and school board, is full of powerful people who want to ensure that nobody else gets their hands on that power, and once you see that and learn where you are in the hierarchy, you have to do something about it, if you have a conscience. You have to do what you can for others. Otherwise, you're part of the problem. You have to see things from the eyes of those on the bottom, or you'll never do everything you can for them."

"You sound like a Christian."

"There are no Christians in America. Anyway, if Jesus came back today, we wouldn't let him into the country. He'd be murdered in a suicide attack in Palestine."

"Dean."

"What's up?"

"You're really drunk."

"You, too."

"You're into Vanessa, huh?"

"She's awesome. Strong-willed and opinionated. She confuses me. I'm not sure why she invited me here, for instance. The logic of some puzzles is that they can't be solved. You know her?"

"Not really."

"She told me everything, man. It's cool."

Connor laughs. Dean's cackle has grown husky from talking. Connor sits on the bricks, stares down at his drink resting on the pavement. Headlights flicker on and off in the parking lot, and throaty engines rev down the adjacent street.

"I don't know how to explain it," Connor says, breaking the silence mid-thought, "but I'm not worried about anyone fucking up my life. Hurting me or using me. I try for the best, but the worst isn't so bad."

"That's some bourgeois shit."

"You're right."

"But what do you want? Like, what do you *really* want?" Dean asks, suddenly annoyed.

"Whatever comes."

"You're drunk."

"You, too," Connor replies. "I'm just saying that I'm not afraid. At least, I try not to be."

"That's good. That's good. That reminds me of something. Did I tell you I'm writing a book? I'm planning it, anyway," Dean says. As he paces the pavement, pulling his bangs as if dragging himself to and from the entrance, Dean rambles through a dissertation on the "vicious iniquities" America has perpetrated, stopping here and there to catch his breath and emphatically proclaim, "Social justice, man." The separation of African families in the colonial slave trade, human bondage, the murderous Trail of Tears, the terrorism of the KKK, the child laborers killed in mines and factories, the blood of innocents in Vietnam and Korea and Iraq and Afghanistan, poll taxes and voter suppression and gerrymandering, the barbaric gluttony of income inequality, and the coming apocalypse wrought by nuclear proliferation and climate change.

Connor listens to the melodic crescendos and sardonic peaks in Dean's speech, steels himself against his melancholic drunk.

"All nations have sins, sure. But the graver, the more powerful the nation," Dean finishes.

As Connor stands and brushes dirt from the butt of his suit, James and Vanessa walk out of the restaurant. "I admire your intellect, little girl," James tells her, "but if you only knew what this country's gone through to kill off the world's communists..."

"Let me guess. You watched the History Channel one weekend and suddenly you're an expert."

Connor and Dean step back to opposite sides of the entrance. Arms crossed, Vanessa stands next to Dean, glaring at Connor. "You two hitting it off?" she says.

"Best friends now," Dean replies.

"Jesus Christ."

James saunters to the edge of the pergola, lights his cigar with a match, and walks back toward Vanessa. "Older folks like me understand. The wagons are circling around us these days, and I suppose it'll only get worse from here on out. The young prefer more and more government. See, the old have seen the worst government encroachments on freedom. We remember when there were *two* superpowers on the planet, so we understand what's at stake and know the world in fact needs less and less government. To be honest, when I was young, I had thoughts similar to yours. I grew out of it. Age teaches wisdom. Be patient, young folks, you'll figure things out."

"Shouldn't have gotten into it with him," Connor tells Vanessa.

"I pray for you kids. I do," James prods them.

"He thinks you're a communist, huh?" Dean asks Vanessa.

"Both of us. Because we'll likely work for the government after school."

"That's where it starts," James says. "I know people who went to Vietnam. I wasn't quite the right age, unfortunately. And my dad fought the Germans in World War II. They didn't do it so we could turn around and tell them it was all for nothing." He looks at Dean. "Aren't you going to stick up for your girlfriend?"

She laughs, a gentle titter, as she runs her hand through her hair.

Dean replies, "She doesn't need me to defend her, but if you think those men died so that a couple hundred families could own all of America's wealth, leaving the rest of us to kill one another over the scraps, you're wrong. The working poor—the real working poor—are the only Americans with any right to claim they're among the living, because they're the only ones who've had to learn how to survive. For the rest of us, politics is a sport, debate is a sport, life and death are sports—"

Vanessa cuts her boyfriend off. "James, here's the thing with you hardcore free marketers. You attribute the hardships of others to shortcomings because you've been coddled your entire life and because believing this keeps your simple worldview simple. But, if you're being honest with yourself, don't you, then, have to attribute not having as much money as the others at the yacht club to your own shortcomings?"

"I've got plenty..."

"Plenty, sure," she continues over him, "but is it enough to shield you from the end-of-the-day realization that you're deeply, irreparably inadequate?"

She and James stare at each other, then his slack-jawed, affronted expression morphs into a devilish grin as he turns and wanders off into the parking lot to finish his cigar.

"Ouch," Dean says.

Vanessa huffs. "Really, though, you two?"

Connor and Dean light new cigarettes, snickering. When Connor offers her one, she gives him a look of revulsion and heads back inside. Once she's gone, Dean says to him, "I think I'm in love."

They smoke quickly, toss their sizzling butts into Dean's empty beer glass, and go in to partake in the last of the night's dancing.

Connor slow dances with Charlotte; hours of socializing have somehow made her more radiant. Even after a bottle of wine and glass of champagne, she shows no sign of fatigue. Not one strand of hair among the nest of shimmering curls behind her head has come undone, and her amiable eyes spring about the room in search of anyone not having a great evening. After the dance, she kisses him on the cheek and scurries off to escort her great uncle to his car and order pizza for hungry nieces and nephews.

When the band announces one of the final slow songs of the night, Connor finds Vanessa sitting off to the side. She glares up at him but takes his outstretched hand, and he leads her to the dance floor.

"You're a real ass," she says, midway through the song.

"No, I'm not."

"Whatever."

"I like Dean."

"Me too. Maybe not as much as he does, though."

He notices her rose-shaped diamond earrings. "Those are nice."

"He got them for me."

"I like him."

"You already said that."

"I'm sorry."

"For what?" she replies.

"I handled things stupidly."

"You should've told me about her."

"Who?"

"Don't play stupid. The girl in Chicago."

"Who told you?"

"Your dad. Who else?"

"It really isn't what you think."

"Oh?"

"But I'm glad to see you're over it," he says.

"I am."

"It isn't what you think."

"It doesn't matter. Dean's great. I'm only here because your dad invited me."

"Same here."

"What the fuck happened to you?"

"What?"

"Your face, dummy."

"It's nothing."

"Whatever."

"I like Dean."

"You're an ass."

"Maybe I am."

When the song ends, she squeezes his hand and walks off without looking back.

Soon the lights turn on, and Connor watches the guests

file out before finding Bill, his ride home. Bill folds the arms of his tuxedo jacket onto its chest and lays it on the backseat of his BMW. He unbuttons his shirt to his stomach, slumps into the driver's seat, and takes a deep breath before starting the car. The night has tousled his hair. His eyes are sleepy. They drive in silence for several blocks, then he says, "Charlotte told me you met a woman down there."

"She wasn't supposed to. And you weren't supposed to tell anyone, either."

"I pried it out of her. It's not her fault. But you should've told me. It would've helped me better understand why you were there in the first place."

"I wasn't there about a woman. Anyway, I didn't want to have to explain things to everyone when it didn't work out."

"I was worried about you. All I want in life is for my boy to be okay."

"It's insulting, all your hand-wringing over me."

"I'm your father." Bill's dimples return as he smiles. His eyes liven. He reaches over and massages the back of Connor's neck, then puts both hands on the wheel again. "Charlotte and I are here for you. Whatever you need. Whatever."

When he turns onto the interstate, Connor says, "I remember this one time when you were telling me about growing up outstate. After Mass, Grandma took you to the nursing home down the street and you listened to her play piano for the old folks there. You said there were goldfish in an aquarium and a bunch of couches. All the people were in wheelchairs or using walkers. Most of them never had visitors. Grandma paid to have the piano tuned, and she taught you how to play, right there. You learned your scales and brought your sheet music, then you went and played for them without her when she got sick."

"Drink water when you get home."

"Do you remember that?"

"Sure. It didn't last long. We got older. Grandma died and we quit going to church for a while."

"The woman in Chicago reminds me of that story about Grandma."

"Old, huh?"

Connor smiles. "Shut up."

"Kidding," Bill says. "But I don't understand what you're saying. Tell me again. Maybe I'm just tired."

"It's okay."

"Get something in your stomach, too, when you get back. Want to stop somewhere?"

Connor leans his head against the window. "Like, I was learning…" He yawns and closes his eyes and mumbles, "*Trying* to, I mean."

"So, what happened? It's over."

"Didn't work out."

"Okay?"

"That's it."

"She didn't feel the same way?" Bill asks in a hushed tone.

"Something like that."

After exiting the interstate, they're silent for a few blocks.

"She thinks we're too different," Connor says.

"Does she have a point?"

"Yes. But she tried awfully hard to prove it."

"So, you're coming home, then?"

"Maybe I'll go to Europe."

"Oh yeah? Just to kill me, huh?"

"Right."

"When do you go to the dentist?"

"Monday morning."

"You going to tell me what *really* happened to you?"

"Like I said, I wiped out on my bike."

☙

For three weeks after Connor's return to Chicago, he and Danielle speak little. The days warm. The wind bites less. With school out, the kids again buzz about the center. Fighting over turf and friendships, pouting and crying, they drain energy from the staff and volunteers. Danielle looks at him less and less, and when she does, when she tells him to go to medical school or work for his father or join the army, he says nothing but stares back at her the way she used to stare at him when they first met: aggrievedly, vengefully. So she stops looking at him and they ignore each other. In their brief moments of shared silence, while closing the center for the evening, they busy themselves with necessary housekeeping, heads down, each contemptuous of the other.

On his next night off work, as he wraps the vacuum cord around his elbow and palm and puts the vacuum in the utility closet, he notices he's alone. He shuts the closet door, listens for the sound of her footsteps in the gym. He looks out back, and when he doesn't see her, he locks the door and checks the office. Finally, he steps out front and finds her standing on the steps, facing the street.

The evening is cloudy and cool. The dried-blood gloaming hushes all. She wears flats and an unzipped black hoodie over a jade dress that reaches the middle of her thighs. He rolls his bike into the center, then locks the front door. In his jeans, plain gray shirt, and running shoes, he walks slowly toward her and stands beside her. She wears diamond earrings, eyeliner, and a touch of cyan eyeshadow. Without a word, she strolls down the steps and across the street, hands in her hoodie pockets. When she reaches the sidewalk, she starts in the opposite direction of her house. He follows her, quickly catches up.

"I like your dress."

"It was Gloria's."

"And the earrings?"

"From Charles."

"Are you cold?"

"I was going for something, but then I got chilly and put on this sweatshirt."

"How did her last appointment go?"

"It went fine," she says. "Let's not talk about that."

"Okay."

"Okay."

"What is this?" he asks.

"It's one night. One night out of a thousand others that'll make us forget it. Thousands if we're lucky. That's how it is in my head. That's how it has to be."

"People might see us."

"Some. Even if they do, they'll forget, too. Or I'll lie to them. Someday, they'll just say we were ghosts."

"And that's what you want?" he asks.

"Yes."

She holds her hand out to him, leaving the other in her pocket. When he takes it, she laces her soft fingers into his.

"It's a long walk," he says.

"Where to?"

He frowns. "I guess I don't know."

"Anyway, they're flats," she replies, glancing down at her feet.

After several blocks, she points at a second story apartment down a narrow side street. "I lost my virginity up there. His mom went for eggs. It seems like a lifetime ago now, and that's what I'm getting at. I could tell you everything about me, but you wouldn't really understand."

"I'd try."

"You would. You definitely would. I've had men my whole life pretend they want to listen to me, when what they really wanted was something else. Funny how the ones who hear you don't want to listen, and the ones who listen can't hear you."

"What about Charles?"

"Charles can't do either."

"Yeah?"

"Yeah."

"What are you getting at?" he asks.

"Do you have any idea how many smooth talkers I've met in my life, all of them smoother than you? I don't believe what anybody tells me, let alone trust them."

"I'm not finessing you."

"Someday, when you've got a girlie cooking for you and kids bringing home their report cards and a house as big and beautiful as the rest on the block, you'll understand what you were up to here. And you won't have bothered to mention any of this to anyone in your regular life. Not Chicago. Not me. Not even tonight."

"That's awful to say."

"The truth is, most the time."

"You don't believe all that, though."

"We'll see what's true."

"You're mad I came to Chicago?"

"I hate everything about it. I hate liking you. I hate the confusion. I hate that I didn't know how bad I wanted someone like you till you came."

"I don't *like* you," he says.

"I know, you want much more."

He squeezes her hand and she pulls a pop bottle from her hoodie, sips, and offers it to him. When the vodka-Sprite hits his lips, he slides closer to her, putting his arm on the small of her back. He can smell the liquor on her breath. "You have a head start on me," he whispers.

"Not much of one, to be honest."

He hands her the bottle and she drinks.

"Why did you have to come here, Connor?"

"The someday you're talking about is a myth. There's no

such thing as regular life. Even if I wanted to go back, which I don't, I couldn't. There's only moving forward."

"That's what you think."

"So, what are you going to do?"

"Finish this drink."

"Danielle."

"It's only one drink. Maybe I'll have another, but that's only two. We'll forget these and it'll all be over."

"You've had more than one."

"I was going for something, then I got carried away."

"You eat?" he asks.

"A little."

"Have dinner with me."

She shakes her head. "Don't worry about me."

"Where we going? We're a long way from anywhere."

She gives him the bottle, pulls away, and puts her hood up. "I know where we are." He looks at her. Her gait is steady, her eyes alert. "What?" she asks.

"For someone who doesn't drink…"

"I can handle my own. I cut my legs up shaving; my hand was shaking. I had to do something."

He says, "If it's only one night, if this is really it, then I should ask you to marry me."

"Go ahead."

"Will you?"

"Will I what?"

"Will you marry me?"

"Yes."

"If we want it bad enough, it'll work."

"I swear, I wish I'd never met you," she replies.

"I'm glad I came here."

"Sure, you have nothing to lose."

"That's not true."

"Maybe not. But let's not talk about all that. Please."

"What do you want me to do, Danielle?"

"I want you to be quiet."

"That's so fucking selfish."

"So what?"

"Am I supposed to spare your feelings by leaving? Or should I wait around and suffer quietly and hope the stars align? Because I don't think I can do either."

"Shut up."

"I can do that."

"But you won't."

She leads them down an empty one-way. Cars line one side of the street. On the other, a lone streetlight, hazy and scum-blunted, illuminates the sidewalk. After passing through the light, she takes his hand and draws it to her cheek and kisses it, looking up at him as they walk.

He says, "I always figured you were telling me to leave because you thought it'd be best for me. But, really, it'd be best for *you*. It would make everything simpler."

"What are you going to do, work at the warehouse the rest of your life? Volunteer and run till your legs give out?"

"I could stay. I could apply to school nearby. Or I could go someplace and come back on the weekends."

"That would never work."

"If you make it impossible, it will be."

She drops his hand to her side but doesn't let go. "Don't do that. Don't try to talk me into it."

"It's all I can do."

"I have the kids here. I have EJ and Marquees. I have Gloria and Charles."

"I'm not trying to be their uncle. I'm not asking you to ditch Charles or live with me. I'm not—"

"You know what you want; you won't stop till you get it. I don't blame you for wanting it, because I've thought about it myself. But don't play dumb."

"I know where quitting takes me, and you're right that I don't want to go there."

"You're so focused on controlling what comes of tonight that you're letting it slip through your fingers. All the pieces you want to put together don't fit. They just—"

"Not without your help, no."

She leads him into an alley, where she sets the bottle on the ground and pins him against a brick wall and runs her lips over his neck and chin and mouth. Reaching beneath her sweatshirt, he hugs her body flush to his. For several moments, looking down at her, he forgets to breathe.

She whispers, "You're not staying here forever and I'm not ever going to leave. Maybe it works for a while, six months, a year, but what then?"

"You have no idea how good six months sounds."

"Yes, I do," she replies, kissing his neck. "But it'll only get more painful from here on out. If we stop now, we'll save ourselves so much hurt."

"How much worse can the hurt get?"

"I bet we'd be surprised."

He rests his cheek on her head. They're silent for several minutes.

"So, what's all this, then?" he finally asks. "Wouldn't it be best if we didn't even have this talk? No dress, no earrings? You could've just waited till I left."

"You're right."

"We'd be wisest to quit now."

She looks at him and nods and says, "But this is the best we can do."

"Okay."

"Stop thinking."

"Okay."

"Don't worry and don't wonder and don't talk."

"You can be some type of horrible."

"I know."

"If you're wise, you're the worst kind of wise."

"Shut up."

"If you're right, you're the worst kind."

"Shut up."

"Okay.

"Shut up."

She slowly kisses his steady, parted lips. He kisses her back, at first lightly, then deeply. He caresses her shoulders and cradles her head in his hands and kisses her chin and neck and collarbone.

When they stop, she smiles at him, eyes still closed, and whispers, "That's better."

"You're a coward," he says.

"A little bit, yes."

"Okay, then."

"You ready?"

He nods and they walk to the nearby bus stop, where they hold hands and wait silently. Boarding the half full bus, she doesn't look around to see who might recognize them. They sit together, watching the cross-traffic and streetlights. She crosses her legs and rubs his inner thigh. When he reaches up her dress, she uncrosses them. They keep their eyes on the passing lights.

She walks before him up the stairs to his apartment. He opens the door for her, locks it behind them, and drapes her hoodie over a stool. They take off their shoes and stand facing each other in the kitchen, five feet apart. He looks at his feet, she at the fridge, biting her bottom lip.

"Suppose…" he begins, but when he catches her eyes, calm and merciless, he stops himself. "You hungry at all?"

She shakes her head, walks to him, and takes off his shirt. He unzips her dress in the back. It falls to her ankles and she steps out of it and leads him to his bedroom, where she lies back on his bed. He kisses her breasts and stomach and thighs and the tiny razor-nicks on her knees.

"You supposed to be good at all this?" she says.

"If it's just tonight, I'll for sure try to be."

Afterward they clutch each other in bed and drink the rest of her vodka, then the few beers in the fridge, and they reminisce about all the thoughts and feelings they've had over the past year and a half.

They kiss and they touch and they laugh.

After ten minutes of silence, he says, "I don't want to sleep."

"I don't, either."

So they cook grilled cheese sandwiches and devour them in the kitchen, no plates or silverware, and once again in bed, she holds him, and he kisses her arms until her grip slackens, and he realizes she has fallen asleep.

For fifteen minutes he listens to her attenuated breaths, then he rises and stands, nude, tearless, near the closed window, absently digging his knuckles into the contusion on his side, until he can think of nothing but the throbs.

"Connor," she mumbles, as if talking in her sleep.

He leaves the window and lies next to her. She wraps herself around his warm bones.

"I'll leave your bike out front tomorrow night."

"Okay."

"And I'll tell the kids you're sorry you couldn't come around anymore."

"Thank you."

"Please don't..." she starts, before yawning. "Don't make this all into something you wish could've gone on forever. Because we both know it wouldn't have. All this love and sex."

"It would've been nice to have at least one."

"Love?"

"Or the other."

She laughs, then says, "You'll find someone better than me and she'll give you everything you need and much more."

"Yeah?"

"Yeah."

"I don't want to hear all that shit," he says.

She kisses his neck. "You'll be surprised by all that she gives you simply because you never tried to take it from her first."

She straddles him, clutching the back of his neck. Then she kisses his cheeks and still lips, drowns him in her heat. The final time is gentlest, quietest, for both the best and worst.

Weeks later, Connor's chunky supervisor Jack arrives at the warehouse earlier than usual and pulls him into his office. Jack sits behind his desk, which he's cluttered with manila folders and blue stress balls. He's mounted his computer monitor on a ream of printer paper. His tiny black eyes dart about like trapped flies. He yawns, rubs them, and, running his hands through his balding head of greasy iron gray hair, says, "Police got us over a goddamn barrel, my boy."

He points to the plastic folding chair on the other side of the desk, and Connor slouches into it, folding his hands over his crotch.

"A goddamn barrel," Jack repeats. "Seems to me people used to get bail more often. Back when I was a kid…well, shit."

"Yeah?"

"But not for what Harris and Marlow did."

"Who are Harris and Marlow?"

Jack ignores the question. With his thumbnail, he scratches the nicotine-stained middle patch of his mustache. "Allegedly, anyway. They were always good to me, so I can't speak to what they say about them, the cops and all. But, then,

I was paying them two, so no shit they were good to me." Jack shakes his head. He pops a cigarette into his mouth but doesn't light it.

"Jack?"

"What's that, my boy?"

"What are we talking about?"

Jack at last looks Connor in the eye. "Harris and Marlow are one problem and you're the other. You're pissing me off. I want to fire you but I can't. Like I said, I'm over a barrel. You been sleeping? You look like this brother-in-law I once had. Got methed out one winter, ended up holding up a liquor store with a paintball gun. Like I said, if you're on something, give me some. I need it."

"Just tired, Jack."

"You're not old enough to be tired." Jack lights his cigarette and sinks into his chair. "Like, you got a degree, and then you want to do this warehouse work even though you don't have to. Makes me think there's something fucked up in your head and I shouldn't trust you, you see. But, then again, you always show up to work. So, what's your plan?"

"For what?"

Jack's eyes tremble. "Fuck's a matter with you, I mean. What happens when your back quits and you been here too fucking long to know nothing else?"

"Just trying to make some money, Jack."

"Fuck that. I mean, really though, when we get up to staff after this Harris and Marlow business, I just can't stomach paying you here when you ought to be…whatever. Get it?"

"Not really."

"I'll fire you. Just know that. And it'll be the best thing that ever happened to you."

"Fair enough."

"Anyway, like I was saying about them two. Cops picked them up two nights ago talking about how they killed someone, if you can believe that. Talking about how Marlow's wife was sneaking around with this other guy. Harris and Marlow are deep in it now. You see what I'm saying?"

"Nope."

"Harris does the second building. Marlow does the third. What don't you get? Three buildings, three overnighters. I got two locked up and a third I'm itching to can."

"Cops got Marlow, too?"

"Don't get smart, you shit," Jack rumbles.

"They got you over a barrel."

"Like I said." Jack sucks a long drag, exhales, and pivots in his chair to turn on the pedestal fan next to him. From the top desk drawer he retrieves a bottle of pills and sets it rattling on the desk. "Want one?" Connor shakes his head. Jack shrugs, throws back three pills.

"Jack?"

"Huh?"

"If you're not firing me, what am I doing here?"

Jack looks at Connor, draws in a rush of air through his nose, nostrils flaring, and nods. "Yep. I need you is why you're here. I need you."

"Okay."

"Okay?"

"I can do all three buildings," Connor says.

Jack's eyes widen, and for an instant, his pupils hold steady. "Christ almighty, that'd be...don't fuck with me. We got a lot of orders to fill."

"I can do it."

"It'd be something if you could. Like I said, you can work for me as long as you please."

"I'll need a raise."

"A what?"

"More work, more money."

"Can't do it."

"But you'll pay two murderers to sit in jail cells."

"Connor—"

Connor scoffs.

"My boy, you really got me—"

"I know how I got you. How long till you can train replacements for the three of us?"

Jack nods, his head spastic. He uses his cigarette butt to light another. "Dollar an hour?"

"Fifteen."

"A week?"

Connor stands. "I'm not on the clock. See you tomorrow."

"Connor..."

"You're trying to triple my workload, then cut me loose at the end of the road."

"Okay, okay, okay, okay, okay. Sit. Please sit. I didn't really mean all that about firing you."

Connor sits down again. "Fifteen an hour extra isn't much with two coming off the payroll."

"Three dollars an hour."

"Twenty."

"Smart-ass. Five is as high as I'll go."

"Twelve," Connor says. "Hire some new people. I'll train them and leave in the fall.

Jack stares up at the ceiling, bouncing his head from side to side. "Eight," he finally says.

"Twelve."

"Eight."

"Ten."

"Ten?" Jack repeats.

"It's not that much."

"Nine, or what?"

"Ten, or I'll burn your buildings down."

Jack's laugh is a prolonged groan followed by demonic snickering. "Let me see," he says, standing, unbuckling and re-buckling his belt like he just finished peeing. "I have to check with HR. No OT. Some might have to come in cash."

"Even better."

"Now get the fuck out of here."

Jack faces the fan. A steady gust blows over his face. He closes his eyes, and his mustache twitches. Connor leaves him muttering to himself.

Every night, from just before dinnertime until noon the following day, Connor cleans the three buildings and prepares next day orders for each, commuting the fifteen minutes between them in a company truck. For a few hours every day, he hangs his sweaty shirt from a folding chair in the spare office next to Jack's and curls up on a reclined lawn chair. An alarm clock radio's scratchy classic rock usually lulls him to sleep. When Jack leaves for the evening, he puts his fan next to Connor.

He drinks water from the warehouse hoses out back. His diet consists of candy bars and tuna he scoops from the can using vending machine chips. "Stinks in there, goddamnit," Jack yells one morning, passing in the hallway. "When do you plan on changing your litterbox?"

By midsummer Connor loses fifteen pounds. He doesn't shower. He doesn't shave. He doesn't look anyone in the eye. The day crew calls him The Stray. One night, near the end of an especially sultry shift, he passes out and wakes up thirty minutes later between two packaged mufflers, dry blood squiggling down from a gash on his head.

Every night, before starting his day, he checks his phone for messages. Twice a week, he calls Bill back.

The new hires are stupid and lazy. Of the first three, only one makes it to a paycheck, but Jack brings on four more, two of whom stick. Connor manages to get them up to speed, taking time here and there to rave about Jack and the job's perks. By fall he loses ten more pounds.

Then one payday, after cashing his check, he throws his computer and a change of clothes into his backpack, showers and shaves at his apartment, and catches an Uber to the airport, leaving his bike on the landing. At the terminal, he finalizes his hostel purchase in Athens, airfare to which was relatively cheap. (He recently read about riots in front of the Hellenic Parliament.) On his flight, the old Italian woman seated next to him, frizzy brown hair sprouting in every direction from beneath her white wool fedora, asks him where he's headed. "I'm meeting my fiancée in Greece," he replies.

"Do you love her?"

"Of course I do."

"I don't believe you."

"Why not?"

"Because you are very sad."

"No," he replies.

She retrieves from her purse a notepad full of sketches, then scribbles his likeness onto the page. Once finished she tears it out and gives it to him. His face, without eyes. "Travel safely," she tells him.

He arrives in Athens at dinnertime the following day, eats a gyro as he follows signs to parliament. He passes a burning parked car and clusters of young men wearing hooded sweatshirts and scarves over their faces, but when he reaches the massive, stately government building, he finds the square before it empty save for trash and pigeons. Police in black riot gear sit on the front steps, laughing. He buys a pack of cigarettes at a kiosk and wanders the streets, striking up conversations with Greek men and women out walking their dogs.

That night he takes the metro to the Port of Piraeus, where he boards the overnight ferry to Santorini. Seated on a deck bench overlooking the blackening Aegean Sea, beneath the vanilla scythe of a moon, he calls home.

"Where?!" Bill says, driving home from work.

"Dad..."

"Haven't you been watching the news? Europe's on fire, for Christ's sake!"

"It's not, though."

"And what about your lease?"

"It was up. Anyway, I can always go back or find someplace else."

"And your job?"

"You think I'm putting this on a credit card? I saved up. Relax."

"What will you do for work when you get back?"

"*Dad*—"

"You *are* coming back, right?"

"Chill out."

It's been many years since Connor heard his father's voice shake. "It's foolish, short-sighted," Bill says. "I've hesitated to say this, but you're wasting precious years fucking around. There are elements to life that you just aren't thinking about. What about your credit score and the student loans you've hardly made a dent in? What about professional experience? Starter home equity? Retirement savings? The world's not waiting for you to get your shit together..."

"Dad, stop it. You'll give yourself a panic attack."

"Like hell I will! I know you think, 'Who gives a fuck about all that?' The fact is that those things are important, so very important."

"It's okay, Dad."

"It's not."

"Dad..."

"So, now what? You'll panhandle Europe, be a gigolo?"

Connor shakes his head. "Gigolo isn't a word people use."

"Gigolo, gigolo, gigolo! I heard Paris is nice. And Amsterdam! I'm sure you could find work there."

"I'm hanging up."

"Healthcare's good in Europe. That's a plus."

Eventually Connor calms Bill down.

"You're already there. Might as well go see the Parthenex, or whatever the fuck it's called."

"I will."

He spends much of the night at an oval-shaped bar on the stern deck, drinking wine, sampling octopus and calamari, and chatting with a bartender wearing a red bowtie. After several hours he pays up and stumbles to the stern railing. He kneels, leans his head against the vertical bars. The ferry's enormous predawn wake mesmerizes him.

On the island he rents a four wheeler and buys a gallon jug of homemade red wine, the first swigs of which taste like soap. There are beaches of black sand as if begrimed with oil, of carmine, with blood. The sea in every shade of blue surges toward him. He finds an empty swath of beach, strips to his underwear, and bathes beneath the sun's suffuse gore.

He buys new clothes at a market, sandals and khaki shorts and a cobalt dress shirt, then freshens up in a public restroom. He strolls the cobblestones until he discovers a small restaurant with outdoor seating. His waitress is middle-aged, tall, with freckles, silver eyes, and long black curls in a loose ponytail at the top of her neck. She wears shorts and a cream white blouse. "Your eyes are stunning," he says.

"English," she replies, shaking her head.

After pointing out his menu selection, he says, "You are so incredible to me, it's painful."

She shrugs and shakes her head again, smiling, beginning to blush. "Sorry."

When Connor's done eating, a cook comes out to clear his plate and Connor notices the woman drinking wine alone at a table inside the restaurant. "You two are married?" Connor asks the man, nodding in the woman's direction.

"No," the cook replies. He grins, rolls his eyes. "Internet boyfriend. America. She says."

Connor enters the restaurant and sits across from her. She turns her head to the side and smiles at him, blushing again. She frowns with confusion when he pulls a map of the island from his pocket, unfolds it on the table, and spins it to face her. She looks from the map to his eyes and back down. With a fork he points out some of the other restaurants he knows, and when she points at him then at herself, he nods. Coyly, she puts her elbows on the table and rests her chin atop her folded hands. She watches a group of tourists pass by the entrance. When they're gone, her eyes flick back to him and she purses her lips as if undecided.

The next afternoon he eats there again, and at eight that night they meet at a bar and nightclub. She wears strappy high heels and a short straw-yellow linen dress with loose sleeves that reach her elbows, her hair coiling down to her shoulders. They dine and drink wine and slow dance and hold hands and take shots and grind and kiss.

Afterward, she leads him by the hand along the jagged cobblestones, around crooks, down twisting slopes, glancing back again and again as though to make sure he's still there, pulling faster and faster, and they finally stop in front of the side entrance to a house.

She flips her heels off and releases his hand to search her black leather clutch for the keys to the door. After a minute she shrugs and motions for him to stay put, then she walks around to the other side of the house. He waits, closes his eyes, yawns. He imagines her dress falling to the floor beside her, conjures the sensation of his cheek against her chest, the sound of her heartbeat. He waits, but she doesn't come to the door.

Just as he begins to walk away from the house, the light inside turns on and she steps out. When she picks her heels up by their straps, she catches sight of him twenty feet away in the darkness. He waves and she winks. Then she steps back inside and closes the door behind her.

The following afternoon, on the ferry back to Athens—where he would explore the Parthenon and one night venture close enough to a standoff between stone-wielding anarchists and their militant counterparts to weep and heave from teargas—he calls Bill to say he's coming back to Minneapolis.

PART TWO

In March, a snowstorm cloaks Connor's downtown Minneapolis apartment in a foot of powder, persuading Vanessa, who ate dinner with him, to stay over. He puts bed sheets, a quilt, and a pillow on the volcanic gray polyester couch in his spacious living room. The sliding glass doors to the balcony grant a tenth story view of the frozen Mississippi, a milky cataract of stilled rage riving the city in two. He lets her use his toothbrush, gives her sweatpants and a sweatshirt.

Just after midnight, cool drafts lusting along the hardwood force Vanessa off the couch. She walks barefoot into his room and closes the door behind her. He sits up in his boxers, squinting to make out her quilt-wrapped silhouette in the darkness.

"How's Dean?" he asks.

She throws the quilt over him. "Shut up. I'm cold."

He pulls the comforter back, she slides into bed, and he drapes it over her. They lie on their backs, staring upward.

"I'm worried we're moving too fast."

"Shut up."

"I'm going to sleep. Don't try anything," he says.

"I didn't last time."

"You did, though."

She turns onto her side, facing away from him, and he puts his arm around her. Her recently cut hair is short in the back. When he begins kissing her nape, she reaches behind her and squeezes his naked thigh.

"Tell me more about Dakota County?" he asks.

"I'm getting used to it."

He takes her hand from his thigh and leads it up to her chest, hugging her.

Minutes pass in silence before she says, "There's a lot of

dead weight wandering the halls. Most of the longtime employees are burned out. Then there are the budget cuts—I feel like a clerk at a store without merchandise. Anyway, I'm serving clients who wouldn't want what we can provide even if we had the best to offer, because there's this incredible gap between me and them. Some are there to fix their problems. *Some.* The rest hate me. And no one trusts me."

"You're an extension of the state. You locked them up and threw their kids out of school or took them away. You harassed them to begin with. What, did you—"

"It's not like Hennepin or Ramsey counties. Most of them are white. What have they got to bitch about?"

"I don't know. Ask them."

"Anyway, I understand all that. It's just not what I expected." She kisses his fingers.

"Then again, what do I know about it?" he says. "Give it time. Before long you'll be another zombie with a pension."

She rolls over and glowers at him, her peach lips and buttercream cheeks shades of gray in the darkness. "I've been thinking. You want to know what's wrong with us? By and large, our generation grew up with as much good fortune and opportunity and safety and security as any in history. So, we're learning more deeply than any before us just how unfulfilling lives of American materialism are."

"Oh?"

"Sex, drugs, and rock and roll used to be escapes for the rebellious. Now they're prisons for the compliant."

"So, you *do* or *don't* want to sleep with me tonight?"

She leers at him.

He shakes his head at her. "Stop that."

She frowns, plays dumb.

"This could be a regular thing, you know."

"It's not, for a reason," she replies.

"It's like we're cheating on each other *with* each other."

"You really need to learn to enjoy yourself."

She kisses him. Her tongue tastes of spearmint. He slips his hand into the band of her sweatpants, but she stops him.

"I have an early morning," she says as she rolls away from him.

He kneads his pillow until his head fits just right. "Me too."

"In another life, you and I would work out," she says.

"Be nice to me; I've been good to you for the most part."

"No, you haven't."

"How's Dean?"

"Goodnight."

Every weekday morning, Connor selects from his closet a chic combination of slacks, button-up and tie, and dress shoes, then drives his red Honda Accord to a strip mall slapped in the middle of an upscale suburban neighborhood. After parking in one of the spaces farthest from the entrance, he walks across the lot to a stretch of businesses segregated by faux stone chimneys and split down the middle by an arched portico and brick clock tower. Between a nail salon and a bakery that lures the neighborhood in with scents of cinnamon and maple and fried dough, he enters the smudge free glass doors of Chalmers Investments, chin high, a newspaper tucked under his arm.

From nine until five, he services client accounts via a single-ear headset, either seated at or standing near his partitioned L-shaped mahogany desk in the carpeted lobby, as he doodles on his cellphone or lint-rolls his sleeves or listens to political podcasts playing on the bud in his other ear. When possible, he leaves his headset charging next to his slim computer monitor and meets his clients for coffee or lunch to discuss their portfolios, advise investment strategies, and ensure proper transaction documentation. Whether out of appreciation or to impress him, they present him with expensive wine, brandy, cigars, and restaurant gift cards. At his six-month review, his boss and principal, Mrs. Irene Chalmers, the fifty-two-year-old daughter of retired founder Charles "Chucky" Chalmers, divulges that she doubted Connor would pass the licensing tests required for him to maintain employment.

"It's not that I thought you were dim, of course," she tells him, standing before her office desk in her petite pantsuit, wearing many sparkling rings and smelling of jasmine perfume. Arms crossed, one shoulder cocked higher than the other, she poses like a TV trial lawyer. "But, as you know, the tests require studying and attention to detail, and you seemed…disinterested. I thought maybe your heart wasn't in it. I apologize, I like to be direct. I find that full disclosure is always best."

"I'm glad I passed, and I want to thank you again for the opportunity to—"

"Bah, bah, bah," she replies, flicking a finger at him. "If you hadn't panned out, your father would've owed me one. Now I owe him. I hope you're beginning to see the good you can do for others if you're willing to listen. When people talk about money, they tell you exactly what's in their souls. So it's important that they have somebody to listen carefully. Also, you'd be surprised how quickly someone, even a complete stranger, will put their faith in you simply because you provided sound financial counsel. I once had a man confess to having killed his brother-in-law over an infidelity."

"What did you do?"

"I bought an eighteen-millimeter Pico Beretta and hid it in a three-ring binder in my desk."

"You notified the authorities, though?"

She winks at him. "Eventually."

"Can I ask why I never see you sitting down?"

Her little eyes, crammed too close to her nose, bug out, and he shifts in his seat. "Connor, I don't expect you to understand this, but in this line of work, and, I suspect, in others, women who spend too much time sitting around are considered weak, and women who spend too much time standing are considered bitchy. I decided to take my chances on the latter. My little halfwit brother, rest in peace, used to work at your desk, and I couldn't allow my father to promote him to the position *I'd* earned just because he had one thing I didn't. You understand?"

He nods. "I'm sorry to hear about your brother."

"Oh, he's alive. I just haven't spoken to him in a decade."

On weekends, he plays racquetball at a fitness center near the U of M and, as spring nears, golfs the circuit of Twin Cities courses with James and Bill. They three make prop bets involving fed interest rates, the Twins bullpen ERA, and whether Charlotte and Bill's baby will arrive early, late, or on its precise due date (December 19th). Connor, who golfs only to spend time with his father, steals glances at the aging man meandering from hole to hole. With ruddy half-moons under his eyes from long hours at the office, and raspberry cheeks from sunscreen-less afternoons on the links, Bill smiles at the trees and sand traps, enchanted.

"You're not drinking too much?" Connor whispers to him post-round, both seated on clubhouse barstools, drinking iced tea.

"Just enough. Do I seem…off to you?"

"No, no. You seem happy."

"I am," Bill says. "Aren't you? It's been a perfect spring."

"Definitely. A lot of blessings since I came home."

"Work is well?"

"Everything is well," Connor says. "Everything is great."

Bill squeezes Connor's forearm.

Connor attends work-comped networking conferences

in northern Minnesota resort towns. He fishes and jet skis, plays tennis and volleyball with colleagues, and loots the mini fridges of lakefront log cabins. He schmoozes with young salespeople and bullshits with middle-age managers, all male, some repairing marriages by inviting wives, some damaging them by inviting mistresses. (The women cross paths shopping at quaint seasonal stores that sell knickknacks, antiques, clothes, and candy.) When the final night devolves inevitably into scandal and debauchery, Connor has dinner alone, then returns to his cabin to watch a movie or call Vanessa.

"You'd like it here. It's relaxing," he says.

"Who is this?"

"Don't be mean."

"What else can I do with you?"

"Really, it's nice here."

"So much fun that you decided to call me? What happened, you got booted from the orgy again?"

"Unfortunately."

"I'm sure they just didn't want to make you feel bad about your performance."

"I miss you."

"I've been working," she replies.

"Put it away for a minute."

"What do you need?"

"I'm starting to think things are getting serious with Dean," he says.

"Suppose they were; why would I talk to you about it? Anyway, if you're compelled to feel jealous, let your imagination run wild."

"It's your life."

"Got to go."

"Fine. How's work?"

She emits a long droning hum and says, "It's paperwork, mostly. Then suddenly a woman on my caseload walks into my office and says her husband came home from the hardware store with three pounds of screws in a paper bag. She was frying fish in oil on the stove. He told her the house smelled. She said he was just coming down and the house didn't smell that bad. He flipped out on her, beat her till the bag ripped apart and the screws flew everywhere. Oil from the frying pan spilled onto the kitchen floor, melted a plastic trainset, just missed burning the boy she was babysitting. She thought she picked up all the screws, but every other day, she steps on one. Oh, and she won't press charges because she can't afford to have him lose his job as a welder and she's worried it'll just make it harder to get her kids back. Plus, she can't babysit the boy anymore—parents were pissed about the trainset—so she's lost that income. That's, like, Monday."

"She wants her kids back, but then she tells you all that?"

"In her world, it's not a story about chaos or danger in the home, it's about what she has to deal with, how hard she's trying to fix her life."

"Think of what she left out."

"I do."

"So, what did you do?" he asks.

"I listened. I wrote a report. Same as usual."

"She wouldn't have told you that if she thought you didn't care enough to listen, if she thought you didn't care about her."

"Maybe."

"No question."

"I have to go, Connor."

"Can we have lunch soon? I'll drive somewhere close to your office."

"Okay, but we're not talking about him anymore."

"About *who*?"

"We're not talking about us, either."

"Okay."

"You know, there are tons of great girls in this city."

"I know."

"You want my diagnosis?" she asks.

"Probably not."

"You want my heavy-handed, no-nonsense opinion?"

"No," he replies.

"I think you're too small for your big plans. Most people would give up if they were you, see the writing on the wall, find someone else. But you get infatuated with women, God knows why."

"When do you want to have lunch?"

While sailing Lake Calhoun with his colleagues, a team-building outing, Irene corners him on the ship's bobbing bow and guilts him into a blind date with her niece Marie, whom he meets for a sunset dinner the following week. The bar and grill in Uptown crawls with college students and tattooed hipsters, yoga pants and bicycles. He wears jeans and a collared white shirt with vertical blue stripes. Marie, a thirty-six-year-old mother of two teenage boys, wears a snug black dress, cardinal-red lipstick, and thick eyeliner.

They sit at a table on the sidewalk out front. She smokes cigarettes and, legs crossed, bounces the suspended toe of her heel side to side in sync with the pop music playing inside. What begins as a pleasant evening of political talk and cell phone pictures of her "handsome little gingers" mutates, after her fourth gin and tonic, into morbid death and divorce monologues from which Connor is too polite to excuse himself.

By dessert, cheesecake with strawberry drizzle, she sits with her legs open, hunched over, her elbows on her knees, drawing figures in the dark with the tip of her cigarette, a sarcastic sparkler she eventually snuffs out in the cake crust. In search of a restroom, she ventures inside the bar and grill now throbbing with bass, and when after twenty minutes she hasn't returned, he enters as well. He finds her arguing with a group of teenagers on the pulsating dance floor, one of whom, a beefy seventeen-year-old in a hockey jersey, with wavy carrot locks flowing to his shoulders, socks him in the jaw.

In the morning, Connor sits on his cutting board kitchen countertop, holding a bag of frozen corn to his face.

He schedules as many out-of-office meetings as possible and, whenever Irene drops by his desk, fakes phone calls. When he finally breaks the news to her that, though he had "the most excellent time" with Marie, "an amazing woman and mother," he has fallen in love with someone else, his workload spikes. She even tasks him with taking out the trash. But he doesn't complain, and by the start of the next workweek, all is forgiven.

Soon his salary climbs. He starts an aggressive student loan repayment plan and a mutual-fund account for the down payment on his first home. He buys a home entertainment system, new running shoes, yoga garb, and dress clothes. Two hundred dollars for baby shower gifts. Another four hundred for Christmas presents. He frequents local breweries and beer gardens, trades in his Accord for a sporty black CRV, dines with friends and coworkers, dates his yoga instructor and another financial advisor he meets at a conference. Following monthly Mall of America walks with plump, radiant Charlotte, from whom he keeps few secrets, he sends her waddling to her parked car with an array of baby outfits.

On a showery late summer day, Vanessa stands him up for lunch, then calls him just before dinner to see if he's still free. He dresses up, makes lasagna and bruschetta, opens the windows to cool his apartment off, and sits on the couch with a glass of wine. He listens to the rain while he waits, and as he wonders if he should start eating alone, she arrives wearing a short sundress covered in pink and Carolina-blue flowers beneath her raincoat. He hangs her coat on a hook by the front door and they sit across from each other at the kitchen table.

"Sorry about earlier. I've been flaky lately," she says.

"It's okay."

"And sorry I was late. The lasagna looks wonderful, by the way. Very sweet of you."

"You look thinner than the last time I saw you. You eating? Stressed?"

She sets her fork down and reaches the fingers of her right hand around her skinny left forearm, as if measuring to see if he's mistaken. Then she shrugs, picks up her fork again. "I heard you're golfing a lot."

"It's basically part of my job description."

"Noble of you to suffer like you do," she replies. "You wear those silly checkered pants and shoes, too?"

"Nobly."

"As long as you're happy."

"I'm not sad," he replies.

"Why would you be?"

"Say, what happened to the woman with the screws?"

She frowns. "Who?"

"The woman who kept stepping on the screws in her house? The hardware store? Frying fish?"

"*Them*. He's in jail. She's in treatment. Everything works in a cycle. Two steps forward, one step back. Two steps back, one step forward."

"You sound defeated."

"I don't mean to come off that way; that's not how I feel. I'm just tired, thinking too much these days, a little spacey. I should've called you about lunch. God, I almost didn't come to dinner. I feel bad that you're getting the leftovers tonight."

"I'd take that any night."

Mid-yawn, she smiles at him, her cheeks barely lifting, then her eyes fall to her plate.

She hasn't touched her glass of wine. "I can make coffee," he says.

"No, thank you. Did I tell you I might go to law school? It has nothing to do with being defeated, either. I'd do it while working. Nights and weekends. The more I'm with my clients, the more I'm able to do for them. Every client's different. Different needs. Different ways of communicating and asking for help. Different defense mechanisms. Concerns and goals and…but they're kind-hearted. Most people are. I think that was always a fear of mine, that I'd start seeing only the worst in people and get jaded. Sorry I'm rambling…"

"Not at all…"

"Is there coffee already made?"

"Keep talking," he replies as he goes to the kitchen counter to start a fresh pot.

She pours her wine into his nearly empty glass, then swallows a bite of lasagna, staring out the kitchen window. The rain has stopped. "There's so much I don't understand. I've never had a police officer come into my home. I've never been beaten or raped or molested. I don't know what it's like to have a suspended driver's license, or go to rehab or lose your kids to the state. I've never even been to a funeral. There's so much I'm ignorant about. It's been humbling to realize that I *can't not* be this sort of snooty bitch with a degree. But I've still been able to connect with people who *have* experienced these things, and that's beautiful to me. It gives me hope because I have so much to learn from them."

He brings her a cup of coffee and sits across from her again. She says, "It's frustrating to know that I could be doing much more."

"Cream and sugar?"

"Please." He brings her both and she stirs them in with a spoon. As they eat, she says, "Did you know that cops can legally search a vagina for drugs? It's rare and they have to get a warrant, which is difficult to come by. Still, from a societal perspective, it's almost more fucked up to think about than cases of police misconduct involving sexual or physical assault. Because there's no ambiguity as to whether sexually or physically assaulting a suspect, even a convict, is legal. An officer would be fired and charged with a crime, depending on the strength of the facts surrounding the incident. But you can't indict an officer for doing, with a signed judicial warrant, precisely what he's paid to. So, however outrageous it is, poor women, typically women of color, can be subjected to these techniques. God knows, the police aren't pulling over a senator's daughter or the homecoming queen with a scholarship to Yale, prying *their* legs open. These girls would evade charges even if they floated around in a perpetual cloud of kush. And that's exactly the point." She sips her coffee, continues, "The law and order folks—well-to-do white men, typically—argue that, if you outlaw these types of searches, women—poor black women, typically—will hide drugs exclusively where cops can't find them. They argue that women who don't have drugs on them in the first place don't attract the suspicion of the authorities and have, therefore, nothing to fear. These are the same people who want the government off their lands, away from their guns. They wouldn't tolerate a day of the stop-and-frisk, search-and-seizure reality of the inner cities. What they mean when they say 'law and order' is 'more law and order for *them*, less for us.' The land of the free is a police state for some, and till that's no longer so, there can be no America."

"It's gotten better, hasn't it?" he says.

"Tell that to the quarter of the world's prisoners rotting in American cells."

"Arch of the universe."

"Not if enough people don't fight for change."

"More lasagna?"

"I'm full. Thank you."

He takes their plates to the counter and returns to his seat.

"Sorry to get heavy with you," she says.

"You've been apologizing a lot tonight."

"Making up for the apologies I've neglected to give you."

"You don't owe me any."

"No?"

"No."

"You act like I couldn't hurt you even if I wanted to," she says. "I told Dean about you, about what happened between us, your time in Chicago. He thinks you're a kamikaze when it comes to women. I think he admires you."

"What do you say I am?"

"I think you're damaged goods."

"Women?"

She looks down at her cup. "Someone told me you were in love down there. You told her how you felt about her and she crushed you, and that's why you left."

"Who told you that?"

She looks at him, her eyes golden orbs lit by the sun now streaming through the kitchen window. "A little birdie."

He finishes his glass of wine. "I have ice cream, too," he says.

She smiles, shakes her head. "Dean and I are looking at jobs in California. He has an offer out there already."

"I don't think you should leave."

"Why not?"

"Because I'd miss you."

"This is good coffee."

"You sure you don't want ice cream?"

"Okay, dish me up."

On Halloween night, he answers the door in sweatpants and a white undershirt, expecting trick-or-treaters. Vanessa closes the door behind her, kicks off her heels, then grabs his head and kisses him as she pushes him down the hallway. She plops her wool overcoat onto the floor just inside his bedroom door, shoves him down on his bed, and removes her collared blouse. Unzipping her skirt, she twists her hips until it falls to her ankles.

"Vanessa—"

"Quiet."

She climbs on top of him.

After sex, she dresses and they sit on the end of his bed in the dark. Not until she kisses him again does he realize she's been crying. As quickly as she came, she puts her coat on and leaves.

She returns two weeks later but is so rough with him, scratching and biting and hitting, that he stops her and sleeps on the living room couch, leaving her his bed.

A week before Christmas, Connor drives to the hospital to meet his blonde baby sister, Melody. Bill, James, and Lisa crowd the hospital room, brushing shoulders as they take turns holding the sleeping infant and kissing the stringy hair atop Charlotte's head. On the way home, Connor swings by a jewelry store to peruse the wedding rings. He departs with an expensive pair of blue rose-shaped earrings, larger and a shade darker than the ones Vanessa has. He wraps the box in white ribbon and keeps it in an empty fruit bowl in the cupboard above the fridge until, a few days after Christmas, Vanessa asks him to meet her downstairs in front of his building. He puts on his stocking cap and winter boots and slips the box into the front pocket of his knee-length wool coat.

It's after dusk. Wet snowfall melts in her hair, clings to her scarf and earmuffs and the fur hood of her fluffy parka. As they start toward the Mississippi, she takes his hand. They reach a bridge along which stands a row of shepherd's crook streetlights igniting flurries in the girths of their glows, like so many meteor showers.

"I'm pregnant. A few months along."

"That's good news, isn't it?"

She doesn't reply, then as they're crossing the bridge, she says, "Dean's going to California. I've been waiting around for him to change his mind and stay with us."

He squeezes her hand. She doesn't cry.

"Will you keep it?"

"I've thought so many different things the past few weeks, like, things I never thought I'd have to think about. Things I never knew *anyone* had to think about. I knew this could happen. All along, I knew. I still never thought...I don't know what I'm saying. I will, though; I'm keeping it."

"I can be a good friend, or something more, but I can't be both."

"I know."

"I mean..."

"Connor, I haven't told anybody else yet."

"Your mom?"

"No."

"Okay."

Her voice is clear, her words rehearsed. "I fucked up and I'm embarrassed, and I could deal with the fallout on my own, the baby and being a single mom. All on my own. But I've thought a lot about it, and if I did that, it would only be to punish myself, not because it's best for my child, not because I have no choice. This is too much to put on you. I just need to say these things...because, well, I just need to... it would be stupid of me, I think, stupid and selfish, to bring a fatherless child into the world simply out of stubbornness. Without asking…"

"I understand."

"Okay."

"Okay."

"And you were right," she continues, "when you said you could either be a friend or a father. I won't ask you to be both somehow."

They reach the other side of the river. She stops and rubs his icy hands. "Take time to think about it," she says.

"I don't need to."

"Really, do."

"I would love being a father. You'll be an amazing mother."

She studies his eyes, draws a deep breath, and exhales. Her shoulders relax. "Okay," she says.

Later in the night, while they talk on his bed, curled up beneath his comforter, he remembers the box in his pocket. When she opens it, she begins to weep.

"What's wrong?"

"Nothing. I just came prepared for everything else." She wipes her eyes and says, "Did it ever occur to you that I wouldn't take these? That I'd never want to be with you no matter how long you waited around?"

"Of course. But people who hedge on what they love don't often end up with it."

Soon, they fall asleep holding each other.

On New Year's Eve he misses a call from Danielle. She leaves no message, so he doesn't return it.

For months Connor doesn't go an hour without thinking of the Fourth of July, Vanessa's due date. In his dreams he smells firework sulfur, charcoal and barbequed ribs, campfire smoke, and the lush cologne of lawn and lakeshore after rain. He can feel the boy's wiry fingers tightening around his pointer, a tender claw. He can see the boy's first smiles, tears, steps. He's certain the boy will have Vanessa's honey blonde hair and copper eyes.

While looking at wedding rings on his work computer, Connor catches Irene's reflection in his monitor. In a tan pantsuit, arms crossed, shoulder cocked, she remarks, "I don't mind the personal stuff at work, really. I planned all three of my weddings from my office, and they turned out immaculately. That's how I won over Gerald's in-laws. He was my second. His sisters still call me on my birthday, and they haven't talked to him in seventeen years."

He spins in his chair to face her.

She says, "It's none of my business, obviously, but if I'd known you were seriously with this other woman, I wouldn't have been so pushy with Marie, which I shouldn't have done in the first place. Being pushy is my sole shortcoming, my cross to bear. That and being nosey. Have you asked her father for her hand?"

"Haven't met him yet."

Her eyes bulge from their sockets. "I see you've planned all this out well. She isn't pregnant, is she?"

"No, not at all," he replies, caught off guard.

She looks around to ensure no one's watching them, then whispers, "I think it's wonderful news. Really, I do. I couldn't have children, myself. In retrospect, I wouldn't have liked them. Most are loud and smelly. But your secret's safe with me."

She pats him on the shoulder and scampers to her office, tapping her fingertips together before her puckered lips, as though plotting mischief. He spins back to his computer, glares at his reflection. Every few days, he finds magazine clippings of baby clothes on his desk.

He informs Bill and Charlotte over dinner at one of their favorite restaurants. He sits across from Melody's stroller, Bill and Charlotte on either side of him. Weeks of sleep deprivation seem to have aged them years. In the well-lit restaurant, he can see strands of gray pulled back into Charlotte's ponytail. After looking over the menu, Bill sticks his reading glasses into his uncombed hair. As Connor calmly relays the facts, Bill cringes, the wrinkles around his eyes flexing.

Connor says, "We were taking things slowly. It was unexpected."

"You're telling me," Bill replies, his voice gravelly. "And how does her family feel about all this?"

"I don't know. Just found out myself."

"I forget, are her parents still together?" Bill asks.

"What does that matter?"

"And her parents, what do they do?"

Charlotte interjects, "You're interrogating him, Bill."

"It's the only way to get information, it seems."

Connor chuckles. "You're worried they'll think you raised a loser."

"That's not it," Bill replies.

"You weren't married when you got Mom pregnant with me."

"That's completely different. First of all, we were engaged soon after."

"And?"

"And what?"

"Second of all…?"

"Second of all, don't change the subject."

Connor turns to Charlotte. "He wonders why I avoid telling him things."

"Bill," she grumbles.

"It's okay, Charlotte, he'll get over it," Connor replies. "It's good news. Melody will be an aunt by mid-summer."

Connor puts cash on the table for the flatbread he ordered, kisses his little sister goodbye, and drives home.

That night Bill calls to offer an apology, his congratulations. "I always worry. Always. Sometimes it comes out in foolish ways. Soon you'll learn about all the worrying I've done since you were born."

"It's fine, Dad. You're going to be a grandpa."

"That's true," Bill says. Connor can tell he's smiling.

"Sometimes we mistake good news for tragedy."

"Well, sometimes we're stupid."

Vanessa is reluctant to introduce Connor to her family. During lunch breaks, they stand outside their office buildings for privacy, apart from the smokers, stooping from the cold.

"I should've met them before they found out."

"I thought…I mean, miscarriages happen. Shit, I should've known. My mom's a schoolteacher, so she's used to being around girls trying to hide it."

"We have to break the ice somehow."

"Not right away."

"You think it'll get easier?"

"It might," she replies.

"I'm going to call them."

"Don't."

"Do they hate me?"

"When I told my mom I might go to California, she was mad I was even considering leaving. Now that I'm staying, she's mad I'm being kept from pursuing my dreams. That's how she thinks. It's just not a good time."

"It'll be fine. Everything will be fine."

"You're not nervous to meet them?"

"What are they going to do, murder me?"

A month later, they eat dinner at her parents' modest suburban house. Pork chops, rice, and green beans. The day is cloudy. The dozen candles of an ornate chandelier hanging from a chain above the table illumine the gloomy dining room. Connor, his hands quaking in his lap, keeps glancing up at the drippy candles, expecting wax to overflow the holders and plummet into the rice plate. Throughout dinner, he smiles at his hosts, compliments the "beautiful home" and "delicious meal."

Her parents, Ginny and Peter, sit on either end of the oval dining table. Ginny, with short blonde hair and hints of a Louisiana accent, is a fifty-five-year-old version of Vanessa. A plumber with a bad back, Peter shifts in his chair throughout the meal. He has a thick mustache and a receding head of black hair. His blue eyes are sincere, pained. Connor and Vanessa sit on one side. Vanessa's older brother, Derrick, sits on the other. A built, buzz-cut thirty-year-old in an argyle sweater, he tried to smash Connor's knuckles together when they shook hands.

"Bank work doesn't really get your hands all that dirty," he says to Connor.

"He used to work in a warehouse in Chicago," Vanessa replies.

Connor, smiling at Ginny and Peter, explains, "I was avoiding medical school at the time."

"How come?" Peter asks politely.

"Wasn't sure it was right for me," Connor replies.

Ginny chimes in supportively. "That was smart of you, then. And now you have a career for yourself."

"Derrick here's in the army," Peter comments.

"Only because they told me the Seals were full," Derrick jokes.

Peter closes his eyes when he chuckles.

Connor smiles at Derrick. "Thank you for your service."

"Frankly, there's a lot I can't talk about," Derrick tells him.

"He means, at dinner," Vanessa clarifies.

"Vanessa…"

"You didn't kill Bin Laden," she calmly replies. "You're a mechanic."

The room is silent. When Connor, staring at his plate, clears his throat, they all look at him. He raises his head and looks sheepishly around the table. "Mrs. Walsh, this is excellent pork," he says.

After pie, Peter puts on a black button-up polo, newly ironed, with a broad red stripe running up the middle and his bowling team's insignia stitched on the breast, then drives the family to the alley. From the backseat, Connor notices Peter's eyes kindling in the rearview mirror as he talks about the league, and as Ginny, in the passenger's seat, gloats about last year's championship.

However, Connor's gutter balls at the alley, which with successive frames are harder and harder for him to laugh off, seem to drain the vigor from Peter's face. Whenever it's Connor's turn, bowlers in the adjacent lanes pause their games to watch him roll.

Eating nachos on the paint-chipped wooden bench behind their lane, Vanessa kisses him on the cheek and whispers, "You can't be serious."

"Why didn't you warn me? I could've practiced."

"I had no idea anyone could suck this badly."

"Can't you miss some pins to make me look better?"

"I'm trying to."

Between games, Derrick buys Connor a beer at the upstairs bar, where he asks, brow furrowed, eyes scrutinizing Connor's, how much money Connor makes, if he has any tattoos or piercings, has ever blacked out from drinking or committed any crimes, has ever been married or fathered a child. By the time Vanessa finds them, Derrick is going over his workout regime and commanding Connor to feel his right pectoral.

"Derrick, we're waiting downstairs," she says.

Derrick downs his beer and rushes off whistling, satisfied with his inquisition.

"Good thing I came before he started showing off his thighs," she says as she and Connor walk hand in hand back down to the alley.

In hopes of making his bowling respectable, Connor goes to the alley three nights a week, sometimes with Vanessa, though only the games she plays with her off-hand are competitive.

He attends Mass with the Walshes at a church not far from their home, as well as a weekly men's Bible study, which Peter leads in the undercroft. The ten participants sit on short in-facing pews arranged in the shape of a diamond. Out of respect for the parish's utility costs, Peter doesn't adjust the thermostat on cold evenings and lights the space with two small lamps placed in the middle of the pews. Darkness shrouds the distant brick walls. The echoes require them to speak in hushed tones, to lean closer to one another as the night stretches on.

"Everyone have a chance to read *Daniel* this week?" Peter asks the group one evening, wearing jeans and his finest black turtleneck.

After the men take turns giving various excuses for not doing their homework, he looks at Connor, who nods, sitting across from him in a scarf and overcoat.

"You mind filling these guys in on who was tossed into the fiery furnace?"

"That'd be Shadrach, Meshach, and Abednego."

"Why were they thrown in?"

"They refused to bow down to an image of Nebuchadnezzar."

"What was Daniel's interpretation of Nebuchadnezzar's dream?"

Connor shakes his head. "I couldn't understand all that."

"Anyone?"

When no one answers, Peter explains the dream, reading many pages of prepared notes, speaking choppily, each sentence linked by ands, buts, and ums that buy him time to find his next phrase. He delves into the end of the Babylonian, Persian, Greek, and Roman empires, and eventually stumbles into conspiracies about the downfall of America and the end of the world. The men scooch to the edges of their pews to be as near to him as possible.

"...The sins of our excesses has brought us to this time of apocalypse, and now we must give ourselves over fully to the ways of Daniel if we're going to keep ourselves from the End of Days..."

When he finally ends his speech with an abrupt "amen," the men watch Connor, who sits with his hands folded, staring down between his knees. His forehead and neck wet with sweat, he takes off his coat, loosens his tie, and undoes the top button of his dress shirt. When he looks up, he sees that they're waiting to hear his thoughts.

"I...I didn't quite read into it all that much, to be honest," he says.

The men's eyes pass back and forth between Connor and Peter.

"According to my research, there's a lot there to read into," Peter replies.

"Couldn't the fifth empire to fall have been...some other one?"

"I don't think so."

"What about the kingdom of the Antichrist?" Connor sputters.

"You saying my research is wrong?"

"I think..." Connor clears his throat and brushes dirt from the top of his shoe. "Maybe, the end of the world isn't..." He squirms, scratches his chin.

He looks up at stone-faced Peter, and Peter grins. "Connor," he says. The men break into laughter. Connor wipes his brow with his tie and lies back on the pew, drawing deep breaths and laughing along. Peter apologizes. "They put me up to it."

"I swear, if Pete brought a goat in, he could've got the kid to slaughter it," one of them says.

Connor and Peter stay after and rearrange the pews to face one direction for the Sunday school class.

"Vanessa told me you bowl all the time now."

"I'd rather not embarrass myself again."

"I appreciate you coming to our group. She says you're not too religious."

"Not really, no, but I'm open."

"Your dad goes to church?"

"Every week."

"Don't feel obligated. We're not, Ginny and I...you know, worried about you and Vanessa, or about you, or anything. You've got a good job. You handle your own business. And you treat her well, which is the most important thing."

"I appreciate that."

After situating the last pew, Peter slouches down into it with his hands on his belly. Connor puts on his coat and sits beside him.

"Vanessa's an atheist," Peter says. "Did you know that?"

"I did, yes."

"I don't know why. Willful, I guess."

Connor crosses his legs and relaxes into the hardwood. "She says God is a fiction men created out of fear and the need to manipulate other men. She says women aren't as afraid as men or as interested in manipulating others."

"She said that?" Peter says. "None of that makes any sense to me whatsoever. But, then, I never quite understood her. It's okay if you're one, too, you know: an atheist."

"I'm not."

"Okay."

"I loved your daughter before she told me about the baby, but when I found out, my love was stronger than ever and I started thinking about our child. Like, a kid needs everything you can give it, a good mother and a good father and good grandparents, and everyone there to help it. I hope you find me tolerable, because that'd be best for the baby."

"Of course. Ginny and I like you a lot. Derrick, too, though he's a knucklehead at times, in case you haven't noticed. When he first heard, the dummy wanted to hunt you down and...well, I had to talk him off the ledge. And Vanessa loves you. I'd say life is pretty good for all of us. Vanessa sat down Ginny and me—Jesus, I thought she'd gotten cancer or something. She was so sad. Ginny, too. 'Oh, Pete, the girl's going to kill me.' I don't get it. If this is what God has planned for us, I'd say that's damn sweet. Plus, now Vanessa's not going to California, either. Then, see, the other day I caught Ginny looking at baby toys. Wedding dresses, too."

He looks sidelong at Connor, who pretends he didn't catch Peter's last comment.

"One thing at a time, huh," Peter says.

"I'd have asked her a year ago if I'd thought she'd say yes."

"Willful, no question."

The men talk for some time, then Peter abruptly reaches inside his jeans pocket and hands Connor a jewelry box containing Peter's deceased mother's wedding ring, its small, recently cleaned diamond glittering.

"Always wanted one of them to wear it, her or Derrick's wife. I'd give it to him, but that train is quite a way farther from the station, I'm afraid. Really, though, no pressure. Like you say, she's maybe not ready for all that."

Sensing Connor's speechlessness, and nervous himself, Peter begins to reminisce about teenage Vanessa, how from time to time she snuck out of the house at night to see friends, how after she left one night he swapped out the spare key with the lawnmower's, then listened to her scratch at the lock until she finally called the house phone to be let in.

"I doubt that stopped her," Connor says.

"If you told her one thing, you could always expect her to do the opposite. Thing is, though, she wasn't sneaking out to party or to meet up with boys, like you'd assume. She had a good friend who was thinking about committing suicide all that time. One night, the girl even took a bunch of pills and called Vanessa. Paramedics said, if Vanessa hadn't found her, she'd have died. Ginny asked her why she didn't just tell us what was going on instead of sneaking around. Vanessa didn't want to out her friend like that. Even that thinking seems backward to me, but, thing is, Vanessa saved the girl's life. Really, what else matters? The girl now has her own business, too, no shit. A salon or something."

"Thank you for the ring."

"Vanessa will recognize it. You're skeptical, but I bet you anything she'll be overjoyed to take it from you. Ginny says Vanessa's never been happier and she knows her better than I do."

In the spring, Connor and Vanessa buy a three-bedroom, two-bath, one story house in a South Minneapolis neighborhood, two blocks from an elementary school that after much research Vanessa prefers. On a sunny Saturday afternoon, the street drains tinkling with melting snow, their families help them move in. Middle class neighbors—Somalian and Guatemalan and Indian and third generation Irish and German—smile and wave at them. Connor and Derrick carry the desks, couches, dressers, bed, and heavier cardboard boxes; Bill, Peter, and Ginny carry the rest. Charlotte and Vanessa stay inside, directing and unpacking, talking and taking turns holding Melody. Afterward they all go to dinner at a steakhouse. Vanessa tears up when she stands to thank them all, raising her Diet Coke for a toast.

Bill, seated next to her, rises to hug her and kiss her on the cheek. "So many blessings," he tells the table. Bill and Peter split the tab.

Connor and Vanessa return home and, overwhelmed by the stacked boxes lining the walls and with only enough energy left in the day to set up their bed, sit on the thick mint green living room carpet and share a pint of chocolate chip ice cream, her latest craving. He draws the dusty blinds over the large window overlooking the street. Two lamps in opposite corners light the room. It feels like a halfway house, as though they were fugitives ready to leave at a moment's notice. She wears her grown-out hair in a short ponytail on the side of her head. Her belly rests in the pocket of her crossed legs. He kneels, ready to jump to his feet if she asks for anything.

"I know you know it's a boy, but what if it's not?" she asks.

"It's a boy."

"Right, but what if it isn't?"

"That'd be amazing. She could wear Melody's hand-me-downs."

She smiles, a smile that to him seems bigger every day, just as her bright eyes seem brighter. Only in seeing her so elated does he realize he'd never seen her so before.

Concerned that she'll stop smiling, he says, "We have a house. A backyard and a garage and a lawn. And soon we'll have a baby. We have our careers. We have money saved up in case of...whatever."

"Look at you. You'll be wearing dad jeans in no time. Coaching soccer and basketball."

"I'd love all that."

"What if the baby has Down syndrome or something like that?"

"I feel like we can handle anything."

"Me, too."

He looks at the blinds. "*Our* baby," he says gently.

"What?"

"You said 'the baby.'"

"I'm sorry. I didn't mean anything by it."

He smiles at her. "I know. It's okay."

"*Our* baby."

She groans as she slowly stands. With her usual droll leer, she leads him to the master bedroom down the hallway. He sets up the bed in the corner, away from the shutter-less window facing the neighbor's. He lies down on the mattress and takes off his pants. She undresses, climbs on top of him, her belly resting on his.

Afterward she rolls onto her back and he places his ear against her belly.

"Your dad gave me your grandma's ring."

"Where is it?"

"I'm actually not sure where I left it."

"Connor."

He retrieves it from the inner breast pocket of a suitcoat hanging in the kitchen. She takes it from him and they lie side by side in bed, her head on his shoulder, looking it over in silence. He watches her put it on her ring finger, on her pinkie and thumb, hold it in her palm and place it atop her belly button. She nuzzles him.

At lunchtime the next day, Bill calls Connor to blab. "I bet it's getting real for you. It's getting real for us over here, I'll tell you that. I can't believe you'll be a dad…and I'll be Grandpa Bill! I haven't been this wound up since…Christ, I don't know! Probably since you ran away to dodge bullets in Chicago. At first, I was nervous about the Walshes. I don't know why, just was. It's good I got to meet them. They seem like a great family. A nice house. Derrick's in the army. Vanessa's an angel, obviously. If you raise a kid to give a shit about others like she does, you can't be a bad set of parents. Charlotte and I are so happy for you. It seems like you're really starting to figure life out. A new house in a fine neighborhood, a good-paying job, not too much debt anymore. No riffraff knocking your teeth out. No working for minimum wage. Now you're really growing up. What more could you ask for? I suppose you'll get married soon enough. We're so proud of you."

Baby shower and housewarming gifts fill the house. He paints the guest room robin's egg blue and lays a waist-high strip of wallpaper around the room, images from the Sistine Chapel. He dusts the ceiling fan, vacuums the carpet, and assembles a crib, which he pushes beneath the lone window, which faces the backyard. He fills the dresser by the door with diapers and baby clothes, the antique crate in the far corner with toys.

He attends Vanessa's doctor's appointments. He chauffeurs her to her cravings. Smoothies, baked chicken, milkshakes, tomato bisque soup, fried green beans, frozen yogurt, hamburgers. Once, he helps her into her tennis shoes and takes her to a bar with a jukebox and small corner dancefloor. After half a dozen slow country songs, she's tired and he drives them home.

Every Friday night, they babysit tubby, cheerful Melody, whose face one week looks to Connor like Bill's, the next like Charlotte's. Vanessa stresses about the temperature of the formula, the snugness of the diapers, the infant's occasional insatiable wails, the tumbles, scrapes, and bonks on the head. But Connor feigns complete confidence in their babysitting abilities and Vanessa eventually relaxes around Melody, who soon hushes only when she rocks her.

One night in the final weeks of their pregnancy, while Connor reads in bed beside sleeping Vanessa, his phone rings, and glancing at the screen to see who's calling, he accidentally answers. He closes his book, slips out of bed in his boxers, and lifts the phone to his ear.

After ten seconds of silence, as Connor reaches the kitchen, Danielle says, "Hello?"

"Hi, this is Connor."

"It's Danielle."

He pauses. "Hi."

"I felt dumb about not leaving a message before. I was going to do that now."

"Oh."

"I wanted to let you know that Gloria passed away. That's all. The funeral was last December. She went peacefully. We were all there with her."

"Sorry for your loss."

"Thanks. Wanted you to know."

"Okay."

"I hope you're doing well."

"I am," he replies. "Thanks for the call."

"Okay," she says.

"Okay."

She hangs up and Connor stands in the dark kitchen for fifteen minutes before dressing and heading out for a six pack, which he drinks while watching TV in the living room.

"You up?" Vanessa asks, half-awake, when he returns to bed.

"No," he replies. "Go to sleep."

The next day he mails a sympathy card.

He and Vanessa wait for the baby, each day a torturous journey in and out of nerves and fear and excitement and dread. They binge TV shows. They take walks around the block and put together puzzles on a card table in the living room. June passes. Then the Fourth. Ginny calls her three times a day. Bill calls him every afternoon. Some nights Connor doesn't sleep. When he does, he has nightmares, permutations of infidelity and tragedy.

One Friday morning, in the second week of July, Vanessa trips over the open dishwasher door and falls to her knees, catching herself before her stomach hits the linoleum kitchen tile. She kneels and closes her eyes, pressing her hands against her belly as if trying to discern if anything feels differently than it did moments ago. Connor helps her to her feet, then to the living room couch, where they call their doctor, a tall woman with a gentle voice. After asking several questions, she tells them not to worry. "You'd be amazed by the stories I hear. You're nervous. Everyone who's about to be a parent is. This is nothing to be worried about. Get rest."

They schedule induced labor for the following Tuesday, and over the weekend he remains within arm's reach of Vanessa at all times.

On Tuesday morning they meet Ginny and Peter at the hospital and Connor immediately forgets everything he learned attending Vanessa's doctor's appointments and reading two books on childbirth. Sitting next to Peter on the waiting room sofa, he drums on his thighs, startled every time another nurse comes into the room.

Ginny sits across from them. "Want some peanuts?" she asks Connor, digging through a backpack.

"No, thank you."

"Licorice?"

"No, thank you."

"Might be awhile, sweetheart."

"Relax," Peter whispers. He puts his arm around him. "Nothing's coming out of you today."

It is at once the longest and shortest day of Connor's life. A seemingly interminable cycle of adrenaline, fatigue, and caffeine highs. He's shaky, queasy, but has no appetite. He nods along to whatever the nurses tell him but can't remember afterward what they said. Ginny holds his hand. Peter talks to him about baseball. When Bill and Charlotte arrive, Bill rubs his shoulders. Everyone tells him everything's fine, but only the fact that no one else seems to be freaking out comforts him.

Then he's suddenly in the room with Vanessa. She's breaking his hand and yelling at him, her knees tenting her gown in the middle of her bed. The stench is overwhelming. Blood soaks her bedsheets, trickles onto the floor. He hears a doctor say "complication," and they show him out of the room.

He walks back to the waiting room.

"What did they say?" Peter asks him.

"Nothing. Everything's fine," he says.

He stands outside her room, peers at her through the window. When they need to enter, doctors and nurses tap him on the shoulder and he steps aside. Suddenly he hears the cries of a newborn inside. He opens the door and the doctors wave him over. "You were right," Vanessa tells him, her voice croaky. A doctor hands her the boy.

His anxiety does not fade. Not when the nurses take Eric away to wash him or bring him back to meet his family. Not when he and Vanessa take him home and lie awake with him, touching his soft feet, gently bouncing him as he squawks. Not when Eric breathes slowly or breathes fast. Not when Connor's heart aches with bliss. Not when Eric struggles to latch onto Vanessa's breast or sweats as he at last begins to feed. Not when his belly and legs swell and his skin turns an ashy bluish gray. Not when they decide to take him back to the hospital a week after coming home with him.

Their regular doctor isn't working, so another one informs them about the tests she will run. Still another delivers the results hours later in his office, along with a heart specialist, a sleepy, ostensibly unfeeling little man with round glasses and an Eastern European accent, who helps explain the problem and surgery options.

"It's a malformation of the heart, specifically the aorta. It's called coarctation. This means that the heart is working extremely hard to get blood through a narrowed aorta. We treat this with a balloon angioplasty. Essentially, we employ a catheter with a balloon or stent to open up the aortic valve. We need to do more testing to confirm the severity and placement of the constriction before we can consult on what approach is best."

After writing everything down in a notepad, Connor says, "Don't you test for this type of thing?"

"It can show up later."

"After a week?" Vanessa asks smartly.

"It's rare, but yes."

"Don't let anything happen to him. I swear to God…"

"Ma'am, we will monitor your child closely."

Bill, Charlotte, Ginny, and Peter return to the hospital. They wait and wait and wait. They drink coffee and talk about the especially hot summer, about the cost of keeping the courses green, about bowling and fishing. They pray together. They hug one another and slip away one at a time to cry.

Finally the specialist introduces them to the man who will perform the surgery. The thin surgeon takes Connor and Vanessa aside and explains in his high-pitched but tender voice "the immediate need to correct a severe preductal narrowing of the aorta."

Connor writes everything down, the techniques, the tools, the post-op necessities, the lingo he later Googles in the waiting room. Before surgery, he and Vanessa watch their sleeping child in his tiny hospital bed. A tube attached to a ventilator covers his mouth and nose. No bigger than Connor's balled fist, the boy's bare chest rises and falls.

Surgery begins at midnight. Connor walks to the gas station for coffee and a pack of cigarettes, which he smokes in front of the hospital. The wind is warm, the sky starred, the crescent moon fulgent. Derrick keeps him company for a while. Then Charlotte comes out to hug him. Between smokes, Connor goes in to hold Vanessa.

"I should've gone to medical school," Connor tells Bill when they're momentarily alone.

"No, no, no. Why do you say that? It wouldn't make any difference. You can't think that way right now. Come on, let's go to the cafeteria. Or else, I'll run out to get you something to eat. What do you want?"

Connor shakes his head.

Bill orders pizza and the families eat in the waiting room. All but Connor, who stands out front, smoking. Peter brings him a plate stacked with slices, but Connor tells him he isn't hungry. The two of them wait and pray. Wait and pray. Wait and pray. Connor throws up in the hospital bathroom, then returns to his cigarettes.

When the surgeon sits Vanessa and Connor down in his office and clears his throat in preparation for his worst duties, Connor's anxiety dissipates, immediately succeeded by something much worse. He watches Vanessa sink in her chair, clutching her face with both hands. She gasps.

For months, Connor wakes each morning to the resounding funeral knell, and his eyes veil with tears whenever he looks at Vanessa. Hers, at him. So, for months, they do not so much as exchange glances. They take up vegetarianism and get a dog, a chocolate Labrador they name Cocoa. They speak to each other little.

One night, while lying beside him in bed, Vanessa suddenly whispers at the ceiling, "If there's one thing that isn't abysmally fucked: my clients look at me differently since the summer. I didn't tell them anything, but they can tell something happened to me while I was on leave. Some of them show up more often, open up more. It's all because they've been here before, down where I am. Like, if I can be hurting this badly, then I can't possibly be the bitchy, arrogant girl they thought I was."

"I'm proud of you. You've worked hard to have rapport like that."

"I'm not responsible for that; it's all because of him."

Thanksgiving night, after they return from their respective families to share leftover stuffing and potatoes, is yet silent, dismal.

On the morning of the last workday before Christmas, Connor dresses for the office. He recently reached another, tighter notch on his belt; the neck of his button-up is unnervingly loose. Were it not for the wrinkles beneath his puffy eyes, his short beard and shaggy hair would make him look five years younger than he is. He brushes the snow from their cars, starts them up, and makes coffee and two bowls of oatmeal with walnuts and blueberries.

Vanessa meets him in the kitchen. She wears a gray wool skirt, an overcoat, black tights, and heels. She's claw-clipped her newly highlighted hair, now shoulder-length, behind her head. She pours them each a cup of coffee and sits down across from him and he pushes her bowl of oatmeal toward her.

"No, thank you. I'm eating at work."

"Susan says you don't eat breakfast at the office."

"Susan should mind her own business."

"Eat."

"Today I'm going to call about the last hospital bill we got. It should've been covered. It has to be," she says.

"I thought I called on that already."

"I thought you did, too."

She reaches for a manila folder on the table, pulls out a stack of medical bills, and begins to look through them.

"Please eat," he says.

She lifts a clump of steaming oats into her mouth. "So good. Thank you," she says, watching Cocoa trot into the kitchen and bury her head in Connor's lap.

"Our insurance should've covered this. I'm calling at lunch," she says.

"I can do it."

"You take the next one."

She tucks the bill in her purse and the others back in the folder.

"I love you," he says, as she puts on her coat and scarf.

"Love you, too. Thanks for warming up my car for me."

She leaves with her oatmeal. As the sound of her vehicle fades, he plucks out his walnuts and blueberries, munches them down, and puts the bowl on the floor in front of Cocoa. Then he shuts off his car, undresses, and goes back to bed.

He wakes two hours later, puts on jeans, a fleece sweater, and a jacket, and takes Cocoa for a walk. On his way to the office, he smokes three cigarettes and purchases a bouquet of flowers. He arrives at the office just before lunch. His fresh-out-of-college coworker Clara, in a pencil skirt and blouse, smiles at him from her desk, next to his, and Irene rushes across the room. "For me?" she says, taking the flowers. "This makes up for calling in sick."

"New pantsuits are too expensive."

She goes to her office cabinet in search of a vase. Clara, full lips, large mocha eyes, and straight brunette hair that stretches to the middle of her back, sets her elbow on the desk and rests her chin on her knuckles when she leans toward him and says, "You heard her, too, huh? Just last week, she was complaining about how no one brings her flowers anymore."

"It's too bad," he replies, watching Irene.

"Everyone loves getting flowers."

He runs his fingers through his beard until Irene returns with a small wrapped box. "It's not much," she says, handing it to him.

He unwraps the present, opens the box, and pulls out an expensive stainless steel watch with a large face.

"Irene," he scolds her.

She touches his shoulder, leads him toward the glass front door. "I also felt guilty; I should've made you take time off."

"I didn't want time off."

"I know, dear."

"This is too much. Thank you," he says, snapping the watchband into place and setting the time.

"After you lose someone, Christmas is the worst time of year. What are you doing today?"

"Relaxing at home, then Vanessa and I are going Christmas shopping."

"Take care of her, Connor."

He buys coffee and a cinnamon roll next door and, returning to his car, finds that during his ten minutes inside he missed four calls, one from Bill, three from Vanessa. He starts the car, cranks up the heat.

"Where were you?" Vanessa answers on the first ring, frazzled.

"When?"

"When I was calling."

"Away from my phone. What's wrong?"

"Nothing."

"Did you call the hospital?"

"Not yet."

"Let me do it, Vanessa."

"Why?"

"It's slow here. No one meets their clients just before Christmas."

"Okay. But will you just keep your phone on you?"

"I will. I'm sorry. You busy there?"

"Some no-shows, but I'm going to the courthouse this afternoon. It's this whole mess. A family that wants to adopt a toddler whose mom was on my caseload a while back. Remember Ruby?"

"What do you have to do with it?"

"Nothing, professionally. I want to scope them out."

"Okay?"

"I'm just curious. Never mind. Shouldn't have told you."

"Vanessa…"

"What?"

"You torture yourself."

"Shouldn't have mentioned it. I know their lawyer from undergrad, so there's that, too."

"You eat your oatmeal?"

"You watched me take it with me."

"I'm texting Susan after I hang up."

"She's out today."

"I'll find out."

"What are you doing, then? Facebook and solitaire?" she asks.

"Basically."

"Okay. You can call about the bill."

Traffic is tight. He calls the hospital. Delores, the receptionist he's spoken to many times now, reiterates that he must call his insurance company. He does. After fifteen minutes, a customer service representative at the insurance company answers, tells him to call the hospital. He calls Delores and demands to speak to the doctor. The doctor's out. He calls the insurance company again, demands to speak to a supervisor. The supervisor, who sounds like an over-caffeinated preteen, tells him his dispute has been escalated to an "enhanced claim unit" that will give him a call back "confirming positive resolution" within two business days.

"Last time you guys said this, I didn't get a call back."

"This time I'm personally taking care of it for you. I will correct this and send you the amended bill. I promise you it'll be taken care of before New Year's."

"We'll see."

"Sir, you have my word."

He hangs up, smokes a cigarette as he exits the first ring of the northern suburbs. Traffic clears. Paved countryside roads abut frozen lakes flecked with icehouses and snowmobiles. He turns into an immense, nearly empty parking lot, puts on a baseball cap and sunglasses, pulls from his trunk an attaché containing his notepad from the hospital, and enters the casino.

The woman vacuuming the lobby, an unlit cigarette between her cracked lips, winks at him.

"Hi, Julie," he says.

The palatial casino is stuffy, tobacco-fogged, reeking of mentholated cigarettes and tart perspiration, of cheap aftershave and toxic perfume. Elderly folks crank levers with all their tendon-taut ferocity. Rows of smog-faded slot machines lead to the poker tables and bar in the back. He buys a double gin and tonic and the most expensive cigar they sell. He sits at a slot machine in an empty row, lights his cigar, takes a few sips of his drink, and reads everything he's journaled in his notepad since he left the hospital. When he reaches the end, he presses the pad against the flashing screen and jots down some thoughts: ...when best to swallow up international equity still falling? Got a new watch today. Now three months without sex. She hasn't left because...? The bills will work themselves out. She knows this. Made two thousand dollars at poker last week. Not bad. She's so sad, she might work through the holidays. Must convince her to see her parents for Christmas. I remind her of him? She hates me for it. Loves me also… Charlotte calls, then Vanessa. He answers neither call and Vanessa immediately calls again.

"Sorry, I was in the bathroom," he says.

"Did you get in touch with those insurance bastards yet?"

"I did. They said they're taking care of it. It should be handled before New Year's."

"They said the same thing last time. I'm calling them now."

"Let me handle this one. Relax. It's almost Christmas, Vanessa. Forget about this one for a few days."

"Those fuckers."

"You're right, they are, but there's nothing more we can do about it now."

"It's an extra ten grand! We can't afford that."

"Vanessa. It's fine. It's fine."

The line is silent.

"Vanessa?"

"Do you mind just—I know it's weird, but indulge me—can you answer your phone? I'm sorry, Connor. I'm so sorry."

"It's okay. I understand. I will. Promise me you'll forget about the bills for now. I've got money. You've got money. We're not paying ten thousand dollars over our max out of pocket. You know that. We'll deal with the insurance people. In two weeks, it'll all be out of our minds. Trust me. Tonight, let's go to dinner. Let's have some wine, plan a spring vacation."

"Okay. I have to go."

His cigar tip glows with each inhalation. The ice cubes in his drink melt, diluting the booze. He tucks the notepad into the side pocket of his attaché, purchases three hundred dollars' worth of chips, and buys in at a table of three chain-smoking, pineapple vodka-drinking men: two brothers roughly his age and a seventy-year-old in a wheelchair, wearing a baseball cap that says, Veteran of Vietnam. Bloodshot eyes make the brothers look like they've been up all night; the vet, all year. His scruffy mustache hangs over his mouth, and the hair on his chest shoots from the top of his fern green flannel shirt. There's a wine glass in front of him full of chewing tobacco. From time to time he pinches the rim with his pointer and thumb, lifts it to his mouth, spits his slobbery syrup brown chew, and wipes his lips on his shirt.

"Ricky, how are you?" Connor says, nodding at the dealer, who wears a bolo tie.

Connor stacks his chips in the shape of a pyramid and Ricky motions to a waiter, who takes their orders and returns with a tray of teetering drinks and two blonde women in identical jean shorts, low-cut black tank tops, and thong sandals. Knowing Connor paid for the round, they gaze unabashedly at him. He ignores them and they shift their attention to the brothers and the vet. The younger woman caresses one brother's neck, then sits on the other's lap. The older, her shy smile hiding a snaggletooth, her leathery complexion caked with makeup, massages the vet's shoulders, turns his hat backward, and kisses his cheeks. She tells him her name is Candice. "But you can call me Candy."

The brothers explain that they're "outstaters" staying at the casino hotel with their families for Christmas. They tell the table to be on the lookout for their wives, a couple of "hungover vixens who look angry as sin."

"What are they so mad about?" Connor jokes.

Up two hundred dollars after half an hour, he notices the souring mood and buys the table another round to cheer them up. Ricky deals the next hand. As the vet tips back his next rum and cola, Connor watches Candice stealthily slide some of the vet's chips off the table and onto the thin carpet, which deadens their landing. The vet sets his drink down, sucks on his rum-soaked mustache, and sees no further than her cleavage as she kneels to scoop up the chips beneath the table. She stands and winks at him. The brothers, distracted by the younger woman, pay no attention to her.

Connor strikes up a conversation with the shorter brother, who runs a kitchen counter installation business up north, and though he tries not to, he occasionally glances over at Candice as she rubs the vet's shoulders and chest, fingering her way through the backpack hanging from one of his wheelchair handles. Connor collects another hundred and the brother sullenly withdraws from conversation. Emasculated by his losses and the drinks Connor bought him, he begins to cast paranoid glares at the other players, especially Connor, and insists on buying the table another round.

The taller brother snubs Connor's attempts at small talk, and after winning a fifteen-dollar hand, he recognizes the chip-shaped bulge in the back pocket of Candice's jeans. When he points it out, the women run off, their sandals slapping against the carpet. Just then, the brothers' wives approach the table, carrying infants. Amid the shouting, Connor sweeps his chips into his attaché with his forearm. He drops his cigar butt into the half-inch remains of his drink and briskly escapes to a bathroom stall, where he thumbs through the news on his phone and texts Ricky for updates, waiting out the chaos.

He returns to the table to find Bill sitting cross-legged on a chair at the end of a row of slot machines. Bill smiles and waves. Connor slowly walks over.

"Let's get some lunch," Bills says before heading out to the parking lot.

While cashing in all but one of his chips, Connor considers sneaking out to his car and calling his father on the way home to tell him he's feeling sick. Dreading the lie, he instead meets Bill in a booth at a nearby diner, where they order hamburgers and fries. Bill wears gray slacks and a pink dress shirt. When he hangs his long overcoat on a brass hook screwed into the end of the booth, Connor notices Melody's spit up stain on the collar.

"You were working," Connor says.

"No appointments. Just some paperwork." Bill looks around the diner, at the empty tables, into the kitchen.

"How did you know?" Connor asks.

"Vanessa."

"How did she know?"

"Neighbors have seen you walking Cocoa."

"She knew I'd be here?"

Bill grins. "She put it all together. She's clever. Sixth sense, I guess."

"I was waiting till after the holidays to tell her about all this. I don't need to be gambling, although I'd hardly call it that. Been making good money. People are so dumb, they'll just hand it over to you. And at least there's some adrenaline, some excitement. Anyway, what's the difference between handling client portfolios and playing poker? It's all tricks with money, how the world turns."

"Connor," Bill rebukes him.

"Tell me I'm wrong."

"You're wrong."

"How so?"

Bill shakes his head.

"It may be a stupid way to think," Connor says, "but not that stupid when you're going to do what you want to anyway. I'll quit if it's so bad."

They're quiet. Connor dries his sweaty palms with the paper napkin beneath his silverware.

Bill says, "Peter wanted me to tell you that the fellows at his church group ask about you. They've been praying. Not about you not gambling anymore, he didn't say. I don't think anyone knows about that. Just pray for healing. He also wanted me to tell you that they miss punking you."

Connor chuckles, rubbing his eyes.

"Hell, Connor. Peter loves you kids. Ginny, too. We all do. All our hearts are broken, like yours, but I know it's not the same. I don't know what you're going through."

"I'm sorry, Dad."

"For what?"

"I don't know."

A film of tears darkens Bill's eyes. He snorts to keep from crying.

"I'm sorry about Peter, too," Connor says. "This isn't what a father hopes for, for his daughter."

"Stop that, now."

Connor stares at the damp napkin in his lap.

"What time are you coming by the house on Christmas?"

"I don't want to be a drag…"

"If you don't, we're packing Melody and our presents up and coming to your house."

"I might be going to Peter and Ginny's with Vanessa."

"You are not. Vanessa said you want to stay in and watch movies, which I bet is code for coming back to the casino."

"Okay."

"Okay, what?"

"I'll come."

"I'm serious. One way or another, we're all going to be together for Christmas."

"Okay, Dad."

They devour their burgers, which Bill cunningly pays for when Connor is using the bathroom. Before they part, they hug in the parking lot and Bill says, "To be honest, I don't give a fuck what you do with your time, or why you do it. I just want to see my boy and make sure my girl has an older brother who's around for the holidays at the very least."

On the way back, Connor spends his winnings on wrapping paper and Christmas gifts: toys for Melody, a driver for Bill, a computer case for Charlotte, and an expensive necklace for Vanessa, from which a ruby heart, Eric's birthstone, hangs. Preparing to wrap the gifts, he scours the house for clear tape, which he finds in a kitchen drawer stuffed with stationery and spare batteries. At the bottom of the drawer, tucked in a cookbook, is an unopened card sent from Chicago. He wraps the presents in the living room, takes Cocoa for a walk, then makes vegetarian casserole and chills a bottle of white wine for dinner. He showers and shaves, dresses in jeans, a dress shirt, and slippers.

He opens the card. It reads: "With Deepest Sympathy." Danielle, Charles, Erin, EJ, and Marquees signed the bottom. He slips the card into its envelope, the envelope into the cookbook, the cookbook into the drawer.

When Vanessa arrives, he's seated at the dinner table. Next to a burning candle in the middle of the table is the chip he didn't cash in. She places her purse and keys on the shelf by the door, takes off her heels and jacket, and sits across from him.

As they drink wine, she picks up the chip, examines it. "I'm sorry I've been shunning you," she says.

"I didn't notice."

"I'm sorry for that, too."

"No, no. *I'm* the one who fucked up here," he corrects her.

He pulls the steaming casserole from the oven and places it on a potholder next to the candle. They lower their heads and eat. It's silent save the sound of their silverware clinking against their plates.

"My dad took me to lunch," he says.

"He said he would."

"I was going to tell you everything after the new year. Didn't mean for it to be a secret."

"I don't care about it."

"I'm done with poker, although, compared to working for Irene, I've been pulling in twice as much in half the hours."

"I wouldn't mind if you didn't want to work at all. I want you to feel good again," she says. "I make enough for the two of us, as long as we're prudent. You could volunteer, coach basketball, work for a nonprofit, or whatever. You don't have a gambling problem—you're just depressed, I think."

"Volunteer? We need to put money into the house. Then there are the medical bills."

"The bills will sort themselves out."

"*You* were the one stressed about them all day."

"Where did you get the watch?"

"What?"

"Your watch," she says, pointing at his wrist with her fork.

He looks down. "This! Irene got it for me. I brought her flowers and she—"

"Thought that little cutie at work might've bought it," she says, eyes closed, stretching her knotted neck by straining her ear to her shoulder. "This is delicious casserole, by the way. Thank you."

"Clara?"

She rolls her eyes. "Could hardly blame you."

"Don't talk like that."

"How's Irene?"

"Good," he says. "Come on, we're going to be fine. My review's coming up. I could ask for more vacation time so you and I can travel. Paris, China, New York, anywhere. It'd be good for us."

"I don't want to travel."

"What else, then?"

She shrugs and pours herself more wine. "Will you be with your dad and Charlotte for Christmas?"

"Not sure."

"Connor," she snaps, dropping her fork. "You haven't cried in months."

He frowns. "Isn't that a good thing?"

"You're not dealing with things well."

"And you are?"

"I'm not drinking and playing poker in the afternoon."

He throws his hands up in surrender. Softening his voice, he replies, "You're right. I don't want to argue. Vanessa, it doesn't seem like it now, but I truly believe that, after some years, you and I will be so happy. When it's right, we'll get married. Then we'll try again for a baby and we'll look back on this as something that strengthened us. Really, let's not fight."

After another glass of wine, she says, as though to herself, "I sometimes wonder if you *want* to be with me. Aside from Eric and whatever you had in Chicago, I haven't known you to want anything, really."

"Please don't talk like that. Everyone told us the holidays would be tough. Honestly, I think we've done better than most would. Neither of us are quitters, so we have that going for us, and we love each other. Tell me about Ruby. How did that go?"

"Parents took the baby home today."

"Beautiful. It'll be the best Christmas they've ever had. Think about that. And it wouldn't be possible without people like you fighting for them every day. Right?"

"I…"

"That's all there is to it," he says. "You're amazing."

She looks up and narrows her eyes at him as if just noticing all the kind things he's said to her throughout dinner.

That night, after making love for the first time in months, they resolve to focus on honesty and healing in the new year.

She goes home for Christmas weekend, and at her urging, he stays with Charlotte, Bill, and Melody on Christmas

Eve. Connor promptly answers Vanessa's "just checking in" phone calls, attends church with his family, and prepares dinner with Charlotte: ham, deviled eggs, au gratin potatoes, and cookies and brownies for dessert. When alone with Melody, she entrances him, as she sits on the living room carpet in her diaper, giggling, reaching for the red bow taped to the top of her head, and as she naps in her crib, the crusty boogers in her nose rippling with her every breath. While watching her open the first of many presents he bought her, visions of Vanessa and their future children overwhelm him so devastatingly, so quickly and thoroughly, that he excuses himself and steps out front for a cigarette. Charlotte and Bill say nothing when he comes in from the cold, or when after a bottle and a half of wine he admits he's spinning too much to hold Melody anymore that night.

After the holidays, a bespectacled grief counselor, profiled by turgidly titled academic texts on the bookshelf behind her and wearing distractingly thick cherry lip gloss, manages in the span of two sessions to tell the couple everything they're doing wrong, everything they know deep down is true but aren't ready to hear. They don't see her again but instead spend their counseling money on a weekend getaway at a North Shore cabin. They cross country ski, dine, and laze in the sauna. He tells her he wants to change careers and go to law school.

Glints of affection in her eyes, which he long feared he would never witness again, build his courage, and on the final night of their stay, while drinking coffee and brandy by their cabin fireplace, he proposes to her. Having left the ring back in the Twin Cities, he merely kisses her hand again and again. She accepts and, drunk on shared fantasies of philanthropy and volunteerism, of supporting local theater and gardening, of purchasing a country home in need of remodeling, tells him she wants to raise a big family with him.

Upon their return, the ring remains in its box in the kitchen drawer, next to the cookbook. She confesses their engagement to no one, and he tells only Charlotte, who replies that he should be "wary of making important life decisions while grieving." Irked, he stops answering her calls.

Vanessa doesn't comment on his occasional afternoons at the casino as long as he nurtures their new goals by studying for the LSAT. He saves up money for their wedding, bartending at a swanky French restaurant in St. Paul. Like his coworkers, he drinks at work and on slow evenings smokes pot out back. The hard drugs he avoids, along with the parties. Every week or so, Clara and some friends swing by the restaurant for a drink at the bar. He busies himself by wiping down the bar, pretends he doesn't notice her looking for him.

Sustained through the polar winter by their mutual, unspoken expectation that spring will be the time to solidify all their future plans, he and Vanessa fall into an enjoyable husband and wife routine. Work night dinners, weekend takeout. Museums, plays, and movies. Daytrips and errands. Lunch dates and evening sex. They celebrate settling their hospital bills by donating a thousand dollars to Planned Parenthood. The next day, while commuting to the office, she rear-ends a Mercedes-Benz, and she and Connor immediately undergo another bout of insurance-related stress, a serendipity they laugh off.

When Vanessa doesn't call him from work for an entire week, he assumes she's put her anxiety behind her, but after one of her client's teenage daughters goes missing and a member of the search party comprised mostly of the girls' basketball teammates finds her in a man-made pond behind a suburban cul-de-sac, the victim of a rape and murder, Vanessa, gritting her teeth and swallowing down surges of anger, admits to Connor that a panic attack caused her car accident.

They talk everything through. She agrees to see a counselor, then balks. She works late hours. Every night, he waits up for her. They talk and talk and talk.

One Saturday morning in spring, they pack lunches and drive to Minnehaha Park to watch the thunderous bludgeons of melting snow crash against the rocks at the base of the falls. As they picnic, she suddenly says that Dean will soon be visiting from California.

"Okay?" Connor prods her when she offers no more.

"That's what Susan said, anyway. It's not important. It's just...he's been emailing me."

"And you've been emailing back?"

"He's been helping me get through things."

"*I've* been helping you get through things; *he's* living in California."

"Of course you are. I'm just being honest with you."

"Same here," he says.

"Connor."

"So, are you going to see him when he comes?"

"Do I need your permission to? He's been helpful. He even offered to pay some of our bills."

"You're joking. You asked him to?"

"No, but I mentioned it."

"How long have you been talking to him?"

"Only a few months. Are you going to forbid me to email him? What if I felt like I needed to go to California to find some closure with Eric?"

"That makes no sense."

"My point is that you're being controlling."

"Maybe I don't want us to lose another one of his kids."

She walks away and calls an Uber to take her home.

For a few days he avoids home. He works, gambles, and picks up shifts at the restaurant, disregarding Vanessa's phone calls and texts. He receives his below average LSAT results.

She comes home late one night and crawls atop him. He holds her. "I'm sorry about what I said," he says. "I want to take you to Greece in the fall. I want to show you the islands. And the sunset. We need a break from all these conversations. I'm worn out."

"Connor…"

"You'll love it. It's so beautiful."

"Connor."

"What, Baby?"

"I'm going to stay with Susan a few more nights. Just to clear my thoughts."

"Okay."

She kisses his cheek again and again. When she begins to undress, he gently pushes her hands away. They lie quietly, and after he falls asleep, she packs a bag and leaves.

He again immerses himself in work. Closing down the restaurant one night, he cuts his finger picking up broken glass. He washes his hands in the employee bathroom, and while holding a paper towel to the wound, he notices Clara standing in the doorway. She wears short jean shorts and a University of Minnesota shirt.

"You okay?"

"No," he replies.

She steps toward him and he glances down at her tan legs and white tennis shoes. She takes a bandage from the box on the edge of the sink and puts it on his finger. "Irene told me about your baby."

"She shouldn't have."

"I'm so sorry."

"Me, too."

She stares at him. Her eyes are lively, sweet. "I have this problem with older guys."

"So does my fiancée."

She kisses him on the still lips, waits for him to finish his shift, then takes him home.

In the morning, walking from Clara's apartment to his car, Connor looks over all his missed calls, one of which is from Danielle. After starting the engine, he takes a deep breath and calls her back.

"Connor?"

"Hi."

"Connor, my God, how are you?"

"Good. Very good. How are you?"

"Fine."

"I got your card. Thank you. Very thoughtful. How did you hear about Eric?"

"That was his name, huh."

"Eric James."

"Facebook. Terrible news. We're so sorry. How's your wife?"

"She's good. Very good."

"I can't imagine, Connor."

The line goes silent. Then they both begin to speak and both stop in unison.

"Go ahead," he says.

"I'd been calling to tell you I'll be in Minneapolis for a couple days."

"I see. When?"

"Actually, I'm here now. Can I see you?"

"I'm very busy."

"We'll make it quick, then."

He hopes she doesn't call to meet up, but when she does two evenings later, he agrees to breakfast the following morning at a small café near his house.

He arrives early, dressed in khakis, a pink dress shirt, and a navy sport coat. Conversing retirees and families with rowdy children crowd the café. He sits at a counter stool with an open one beside it and orders coffee. While he sips, he reads a newspaper left by another customer and peruses a menu he already knows well. After five minutes, he glances around the café and finds her standing by a corner table along a wall of windows facing a busy street. A broad olive headband, knotted at the top of her head, bunches her curls behind her head and draws out her mascaraed eyes. In sneakers, faded jeans, and a Chicago Bears shirzee, she holds a car seat in one arm and a wooden highchair and tan tote bag in the other. The host carries away the chair nearest the window and Danielle skillfully overturns the highchair so its four legs point upward, then places the car seat securely atop it. She pushes the accordion-style cover back, peaks inside at the sleeping baby, and pulls the cover back over the seat.

As he nears, she catches sight of him. Her eyes widen in shock, as if she didn't expect him to show up. She hugs him from the side, resting her head on his shoulder for an instant. "Look at these clothes," she says as she tugs on his lapel.

Sunlight beats on the window. He removes his coat and hangs it from the back of his chair before sitting down. He eyes the car seat.

"I was going to leave her with my aunt today, but I changed my mind. Connor, this is my daughter, Cecelia."

"Is she asleep?"

"It's okay," she says, inching the cover back.

He crouches beside the highchair, peering at Cecelia's eyelids and lashes, her chubby cheeks and the thin curls atop her head.

"You see those pimples on her forehead," Danielle says. "She's breaking out from the heat a little."

"We can wait for another table, or go somewhere else."

"She'll be fine."

"Will she be able to sleep here? Is it too loud?"

"She's okay, Connor."

They order orange juices and omelets. A server brings him the cup of coffee he forgot at the counter.

"I don't think she looks like you."

"Everyone says she looks more like Charles."

"How *is* Charles?"

"Charles is Charles. He's out on his own again."

"I'm sorry to hear that."

"He wanted me to tell you we prayed for you. The boys, too. We've all been thinking of you."

"That's nice of you all."

"When I heard…" She shakes her head, biting her lower lip.

"How's the center?"

"It closed. Budget cuts."

"No."

"Now I work as a paraprofessional at EJ's school. It's managing behaviors, like I did at the center. I'm paid better now, though. Even bought Gloria's house for myself, and a car."

"Sounds like everything's going great."

She tells him she's in town to see her aunt and uncle. "They're getting up there and they're trying to get rid of some stuff in their house, so I'm helping them with a garage sale. Thought I'd call you up."

She bows to sip orange juice through her straw, then pops her head up. "Ah! I almost forgot." She digs through her bag for an envelope, hands it to Connor. "Marquees made you something."

He unfolds the piece of paper inside, a colored pencil drawing of a boy and a man standing side by side.

"That's Marquees in the LeBron jersey, you in the Jordan jersey."

"I see. Very sweet of him." He folds the drawing up, tucks it into the inner pocket of his coat.

"I thought I'd meet her," she says.

"Who?"

"Your wife?"

"We're not married. Anyway, she's busy today, unfortunately."

"That's too bad."

They go silent and she says, "Maybe this is weird."

"Not at all. Why would it be?"

"No reason. Although, I have to come clean about something. I didn't learn about your baby from Facebook. It was your stepmom."

"You talked to Charlotte?"

"A few times. We mostly text. I was worried, but I didn't want to bother you. Charlotte's great."

"She is."

"Maybe that was creepy of me."

He finishes his cup of coffee and looks around for the waiter. "I'm sure it came from the right place. What else did she tell you?"

"What do you mean?"

He shrugs. They glance at Cecelia as she stretches her head out but doesn't wake.

"She told me your job's going well."

"Everything is wonderful here. It was rough for a while, but I'm back on track these days. Vanessa and I are engaged. We have a dog. Look at me, I'll be thirty soon and I'm fattening up like I'm supposed to." He pats his belly.

The waiter brings their omelets and Cecelia begins to squawk. Danielle only takes two bites before she picks her daughter up and, gently bouncing her, carries her to the quiet café entrance. He looks at the empty car seat. A waitress fills his coffee cup. He doesn't pick his fork up until Danielle comes back and lays sleeping Cecelia down in her car seat.

They eat, heads down. Here and there he glances up at

Danielle. Sunlight gleams on her cheeks, exposing her nascent crow's feet creases. "I slept with a coworker last night," he suddenly says. Danielle sits up straight, swallows her bite. "I think Vanessa's going to California to be with Dean. She's always been in love with him."

"Who's Dean?"

"I'm sorry, that's Eric's father."

"Eric? Your *son*, Eric? I mean…"

He nods. "I've been working two jobs, gambling on the side, drinking too much. But I'm ahead on my mortgage and have enough saved up in case everything goes to hell, which God knows, it will. There, now you don't have to wait to hear it from Charlotte."

She glowers at him, then looks down at her plate. "I didn't know all that. I could tell you didn't want to do this," she says softly.

"I don't see what good it's doing you, either. I'll pay for breakfast."

"I already did."

"Even better."

"I'm not done eating, though," she says.

"Me, neither. Might even get more coffee."

"I'll call the waiter over for you."

"Still stubborn, huh?"

"And you're different now that your shirts have buttons?"

"I…" He stops himself.

"What?"

"Never mind. I don't care," he says.

"Yes, you do. So do I."

Though the café clamor drowns out their raised voices, those at the tables nearest them, sensing drama, begin to listen in and watch them from the corner of their eyes.

"I'm sorry if this isn't going like you'd hoped. Sorry if you're embarrassed by me," he says.

"Do I seem embarrassed?"

"No."

"Anyway, that's not what you were going to say."

"What was I going to say?"

"Not that," she replies.

"Why are you here?"

"Checking in on a friend."

"Can this be the last time, please?"

"If that's what you want."

He leans in and lowers his voice. "I don't know you and I don't really want to anymore. Do I answer your calls? Respond to your texts? What, should I feel blessed by your sudden consideration for me?"

"It's not sudden," she whispers.

"What?"

"I said, 'It's not sudden.' But I'm not here to go over all that."

"Me, neither. I came to tell you that I don't want you to contact me again."

"I won't, then."

"Good. Thank you," he replies.

"Could've said that on the phone, saved us a scene."

"I didn't think it through."

"I shouldn't have brought Cecelia."

"She has nothing to do with it. I just—"

"It's okay, Connor. You don't have to explain."

"I want to."

She looks at him, waiting, but he merely takes the last bite of his omelet and stares out the window. He finishes his second cup of coffee and says, "It's not personal. I don't want to see anyone."

She waits for him to continue. When he doesn't, she adjusts her headband and peaks in on Cecelia. Then she asks, "What *do* you want?"

"Wanting has never done me any favors."

"Okay? What are you going to do?"

"About what?"

"About *living*?"

"Charlotte already told you: my job's going well. And I got a dog."

"That's enough for you?"

"She's a good dog."

For the first time today she laughs, a delicate, mirthful chitter he recognizes. "I doubt it will be," she says.

"Why not?"

"Right—I know nothing about you. You've completely changed into a completely different person."

"Yes and no."

She finishes her omelet and juice. He starts his third cup of coffee.

"Damn, this coffee's burnt. So, you think you fucked up back then, is that it?"

"No. I did what was best at the time. You know, *you* could've called *me*," she replies.

"You said not to."

"I said a lot of things."

He scratches his neck, yawns. "Well, it's all over now. Tell me more about your job."

"I did what was best."

"Fine, you're perfect. *I'm* the screw-up."

"I didn't say that."

"It's okay, I don't care. Life's too short. How are the boys?"

"You knew what you were asking me to do."

"All in all, you were asking as much of me as I was of you. But it doesn't matter. Let's move on. I don't want to rehash—"

"You don't?"

He shakes his head, his lips downturned.

She grins at him. "Fine, then."

"Good."

"Connor, you look fatter."

"And you look older," he retorts.

"I am."

"That must be it, then."

She talks about her battles with the teachers and administrators who are quick to kick kids out of her school, including EJ, now twelve years old. He has gotten into some scraps and is hanging out with older kids who "have nothing going on."

When Cecelia wakes, Connor asks if he can hold her. They three leave the café, and for fifteen minutes Connor cradles Cecelia on a bus stop bench in the shade of an elm tree, again and again kissing the top of her head. Then he and Danielle hug goodbye.

"Stay in touch, if you want to," she tells him.

Looking at Cecelia in her car seat, he smiles but says nothing.

He slips Marquees' drawing into the cookbook in the kitchen, then braces for the drama he's sure the following weeks will bring him.

On Monday, Irene drops a twenty-pound stack of folders on his desk, assigning him the office's neediest, most aggrieved clients. Later, when he takes his watch off to rub his wrist and leaves it unattended at his desk, she takes it back. So, Connor is unsurprised when Vanessa learns about his night with Clara. The news aggravates Vanessa, not enough to confront Connor but enough to let it slip to Derrick, who, after leaving Connor some threatening phone messages, informs Peter and Ginny. By the time Connor sees Vanessa again the next weekend, it seems to him his coworkers and neighbors have recycled enough rumors to turn him into the most heinous man on earth. She neither apologizes nor asks him to, but informs him that she'll be staying in Susan's guest room indefinitely.

He spends his evenings gambling, drinking with strangers, and golfing with James, whose retirement has fostered crueler, more belligerent exposés on free market solutions to healthcare and immigration. Connor wants to call Peter, but doesn't. He wants Vanessa to officially move out, but won't ask her to. He wants to tell everyone the baby wasn't his, but refrains. He gets kicked out of a bar over an argument about gun control, then returns the next night to argue with someone else, taking the exact opposite position, and gets kicked out again. He buys a two-thousand-dollar bike, an eight-hundred-dollar pair of skis, and a four-hundred-dollar used dirt bike. He stops taking Cocoa for walks, so she defecates in the clothes hamper and under the kitchen table. He buys a video game console and stays in all weekend, smoking weed and ordering subs. He gets whooped by teenagers whose avatars are StrokeLord and FeistyGinger19. Then he takes the console back to the store two days later, argues with a clerk about the store's return policy.

One night Vanessa calls to tell him she took another job and will be moving away in six weeks.

"What about your clients?"

"There are clients everywhere."

"I suppose…"

"You don't want me to stay here," she says. "This is a good thing."

"Okay. The job's in California?"

"Cleveland."

"Not the same thing."

"Not at all."

"I'm so sorry for everything, Vanessa."

"It's not all your fault."

"I love you."

"I love you, too. I'm not mad, either. I feel like I'm holding you back."

"From what?" he asks, incredulous.

"I guess you'll find out someday."

Clara invites him to a party at her college roommate's townhouse, and from the moment he arrives, an hour early, already buzzing, he realizes he's made a huge mistake. He drinks four beers alone by a backyard fire pit, then a gang of jocks and college girls arrives. When the sun sets, the boys light a bonfire and tear up the grass with inebriated lawn games. Soon, their sidelong smirks at Connor evolve into a full-on roast of "Uncle C's" desire for Clara, his "dad tennis shoes," his too-loose jeans and too-tight dress shirt. Clara eventually shows up but stays for only ten minutes before departing with a lacrosse player, and Connor sticks around for another masochistic half-hour, drinking his fill and laughing off their slights, before taking an Uber home. In a pit-stained undershirt, he stands before his bathroom mirror, sucking his gut in and pushing it out.

He sleeps in late, showers, and heads to work at the restaurant. At the end of a quiet shift, he slips out back for a smoke and returns to find Charlotte seated at the end of the otherwise empty bar, wearing pajama bottoms, running shoes, and a hooded raincoat.

"Would you like to see a menu?" he asks cheerily.

"No, thank you."

"Wine list? On tap we have—"

"Not thirsty," she interrupts him.

"You look like a Sith. When did it start raining?"

"What's going on with you?" she whispers, pulling back her hood.

"What do you mean?"

"Connor."

"And why are you wearing pajamas?"

"Your dad doesn't know I'm here. All things equal, I'd rather he not."

"You snuck out?"

"I keep telling him not to worry about you, so I don't want him to know how much I am."

"You two are ridiculous."

She runs her hands through her hair. Her narrowed eyes, swollen from motherhood stressors and long hours at work, spook him—he's never seen her so angry.

He says, "Is this about Clara and Vanessa? Because that's all over with, everyone's moving on."

"It's about you," she replies, her voice calm.

"It was a mistake. Did Vanessa tell you she's leaving for Cleveland?"

"I'm not asking about her."

"I don't know what to say, Charlotte. I'm…" He shakes his head as he leaves to fill a drink order.

When he returns, she says, "I know Eric wasn't yours."

He pauses. "He was my son."

"Of course he was, but Vanessa told me about what's-his-face."

"Why'd she do that?"

"Don't ask me. She told me after he died. Guilt, maybe."

"Whatever. It's all over now."

Exasperated, she taps her fingernails on the wooden bar, takes a deep breath. He stares across the restaurant at an old couple coming in from the rain. She says, "I don't understand how the man who did that for her, for your son, can stomach all the stupid bullshit you're doing now."

"It was *one* night."

"I don't care about that. Why are you spending so much time with my father?"

"I love your dad."

"Not as much as I do, but if you end up like him, I'll murder you."

"He's just loud," he replies.

"He's an asshole."

"You think I'm an asshole?"

"Seems it's what you're going for."

"He's a good guy."

"He is what he is; you're better than that."

"I see what you're up to. Do me a favor and please stop talking to Danielle. She doesn't need a briefing every time I screw up. I grew up without a mom; now I have more of them than I can handle."

"I thought she could help you. If I think she can in the future, I'll drive her up from Chicago myself."

"Just focus on your kid, would you?"

"I am."

He bites his thumbnail. She raps the edge of her cell phone on the bar top.

"Believe it or not, things are going well for me," he says, filling another order.

"No, they're not."

"If it makes you feel better, I'll tell you I'm even thinking of volunteering with a youth basketball league. Or else, I might apply to law school in the fall. Did Vanessa ever tell you about how the police can get a warrant to search a woman's…you know? It's not right."

"You're fucking hilarious."

"I'm being serious."

"Clearly, not serious enough."

"Charlotte—"

She points her phone at him and raises her voice. "I'll keep calling you, and if you continue to not answer, I'll continue showing up here. And if you get another job, I'll show up there. I'll keep bothering you till you get your shit together.

You want help with your résumé or an application, I'll help. You want to talk through career options or need a ride to volunteer at a soup kitchen, anything. But, if I can help it, you will not be bartending and gambling four times a week much longer."

A nearby waitress raises her head. Connor's manager, a bony twenty-four-year-old with fifteen earrings and long black hair in a man-bun, skulks over to observe.

Noticing him, Charlotte backtracks. "No offense. It's a fine job, just not for him."

She flips her hood over her head. The manager follows her to the door. "Everything okay tonight, ma'am?"

"Your bartender's a prick. You should fire him," she replies as she exits.

Connor and Vanessa put the house on the market. He gives Irene two weeks' notice, and after a week of scowling at Cocoa and warding off Charlotte's nightly calls with the repeated claim that he's "thinking things over," he sends her the confirmation emails for his online applications to seven law schools in the Midwest, three in Minnesota. He sells off the toys he recently purchased and mischievously offers Cocoa to Bill and Charlotte, aware of her tendency to lick Melody's hair into spikes after they bathe her. A compromise, Charlotte begrudgingly agrees to take the dog.

Only two schools accept him, one in Iowa, the other in Chicago. When he has Bill and Charlotte over for dinner to tell them he's leaving in the fall, she jumps up from the table, hugs him, and cries, "Oh, Connor, we're so happy for you. What a great surprise! What finally made you decide to follow through?"

"Too bad you didn't get in to any schools close by," Bill says.

"Which will you choose?" she asks.

"Might be nice to go somewhere I've never been. Start over. The basic curriculum's the same."

"Go to Chicago."

"Why?" Bill asks. "Last time, he never came back to see us."

"He already knows some people there."

"I'll meet new people."

"Starting over is hard. Anyway, you're not a cornfields guy."

Bill pleads, "Wherever you go, would you at least live in a nice area where we three can visit you? Please?"

"It won't be like last time, Dad. You'll see me as much as you do now."

"It's settled," Charlotte says, folding her hands before her chin. "An excellent decision! My boy, my boy!"

Connor smiles at her, and Bill looks suspiciously at them, then shrugs.

A newlywed couple purchases Connor and Vanessa's house. Peter rents a trailer to pick up the rest of her belongings plus everything the new homeowners don't want as part of the sale, the dishware, entertainment system, furnishings, and kitchen table. While packing, the Walshes pretend Connor isn't there. Derrick tells him not to help but doesn't object when Peter's back pain compels Connor to carry boxes to the lawn. While the Walshes eat ordered pizza by the trailer, Connor has a ham sandwich in the kitchen, chatting with Vanessa.

"Chicago's not far from Cleveland, if you ever want to visit," he says.

"Maybe. You never know."

Peter and Derrick do one last sweep through the house, then she and Connor hug goodbye. On his way out, Peter squeezes Connor on the shoulder. "Take care," he says.

Awaiting his move-in date, he stays with Bill and Charlotte

for a week, his things packed in his car. Melody toddles around the house, throwing toys, fussing, and yammering. He takes her for walks around the block in her stroller and naps with her on the living room recliner. All through the morning of his departure, he holds her. When Charlotte finally pries her away, Melody's tiny fingers, grubby from playing with him in the yard that morning, clutch his shirt sleeve. Driving south, he notices the smudged prints. He cries.

With only a carload of things to lug up to his second story studio apartment two blocks from campus, the move goes quickly. A bathroom, a tidy living room with a bed, a kitchenette. Midway through assembling a new shelf for his textbooks, he stops to drink a glass of water and rub his neck. His phone rings.

He sighs but answers. "Didn't expect to hear from you."

"I know," Danielle replies.

"I'm sure you heard already, but I'm back in Chicago. I was going to call you. I didn't want to run into you and have you think I was avoiding you."

"Chicago's a big city."

"With my luck…"

"Worse things could happen to you," she says. "Law school, huh? That's great."

They're silent. He tickles his chin with his fingertips and says, "Can you do something for me? I don't want anything but school. Don't get me wrong, it was wonderful to see you and Cecelia—"

"It's okay," she interjects. "I just want to welcome you. If you need anything, you have my number."

"Okay. Everything good there?"

"You really want to know?"

"Just this time."

"EJ was picked up by the police yesterday."

"For what?"

"They said they got him on camera, said he was involved in a riot. Some other boys got beat up pretty bad. One got stabbed. EJ will be in detention for a month before trial."

"That's a long time, especially at the end of summer."

"If you plead guilty, you get released right away, but you'll have it on your record. If you don't, you have a shot at trial and a clean record, but you have to wait for it. He told Erin he didn't do anything, so she won't let him plead guilty like his friends did."

"I'm sure he likes that," he says.

"Nephew's going to be bored as hell. I'm going to see him in a couple days."

"I'll be thinking of him. Tell him I said that, if it means anything to him."

"It will. He won't show it, though. He wants everyone to know how tough he is."

A week passes. On the eve of the first day of classes, he joins hundreds of his first year classmates for a commencement gala in a sprawling campus ballroom lit by six identical chandeliers. Waiters in tuxedos and bowties serve champagne, crab cakes, and bacon-wrapped shrimp. Heavy forest green linen adorns forty circular high top dining tables. Pregnant couples show off extravagant wedding rings. Professors in matching blazers tell stories and answer curriculum questions. While listening to an anxious, shrill young man explain to him in detail why he didn't enroll at a more prestigious school, Connor excuses himself and, secluded beneath a side exit archway, texts Danielle: *where they keeping EJ?*

PART THREE

Minutes into Monday morning's ninth grade math class, Mr. Griffin calls the paraprofessionals' office and asks for Danielle. When she arrives moments later in her dark navy work polo, she doesn't take her usual seat on the back corner stool. Instead, she stands in the doorway, using her foot to prop the door open behind her, and watches fifteen-year-old Tevon, deliberately seated close to the door, rise from his desk with his fists clenched beside him.

Mr. Griffin sits behind his desk in front of the class, as Tevon shouts at him, "What did you call her for? I didn't do anything! I'm going to treat your ass! How about that? I swear to God. Treat your ass, man, like a stepkid! I didn't do anything!" A chunky, baby-faced boy with slightly crossed brown eyes, he turns to Danielle, slamming his right fist into his open left palm. "Swear to God, Danielle. I'm treating that man's ass! He told you I did something? I didn't! I swear to God!"

Mr. Griffin, a head taller than Tevon, his neck and shoulders brawny, calmly strokes his trimmed beard with his fingers. He silences two giggling students with a shake of his head, then glances over at Danielle, who, taking a step back to open the door wide, says to Tevon, "Your uncle called. I've got some news for you. Let's go."

"I'm not leaving this room till I treat that ass," he replies, pointing at Mr. Griffin. "Swear. To. God. A man's ass has never been treated so bad as I'm about to. He's always doing this to me for no reason. I—" Tevon abruptly stops when Mr. Griffin walks out from behind his desk, scowling at him. The kids laugh and Tevon smirks for a moment before straightening his face. Mr. Griffin leans back against the chalkboard.

As he walks toward Danielle and backs out of the room, Tevon says, "I swear. I'm only going because of my uncle.

When I come back, it's going to be nightie-night for you, Griff. Treat. That. Ass."

When Tevon stops to beat his chest with his fists and crow like a rooster, the classroom again breaks into laughter. Danielle grabs the back of his shirt and pulls him out of the room.

They walk down the empty hallway.

"Proud to clown around like that?"

"Wasn't clowning," he replies.

"What's going on?"

"Nothing. What'd my uncle have to say?"

"He didn't call. I was just getting you out of there before you got kicked out."

"Griff should thank you. You saved his life."

"Don't joke like that."

"He's always pulling shit on me."

"He did you a favor. He should've called the principal again."

"Where we going?"

"For a walk."

"I'm telling you, I'm not going back to class."

"Yes, you are."

"It's a waste of time. Got other shit to do, anyway."

"You think I don't? I have fifty Tevons in this school, all acting like you, trying to make it their last day here."

"There's only one Tevon," he replies, winking at her.

"What's going on?"

"Nothing."

"Don't give me that."

They pass two girls texting in front of an open locker. "Oh my God," Danielle says in a whiny, high-pitched voice. "I can't believe she said that about Monica."

They giggle. "Shut up, Danielle," one of them says.

"Go to class."

"Okay," the girl replies, shutting the locker. The girls walk toward their classroom.

"What is it?" she asks him again.

"Why do you care?"

"I'm nosey."

"I'm not telling you."

"Fine. See what your reports look like at the end of the week."

"You can't do that," he wails.

"I run this school."

"See how tough you are on the outs."

"I run those, too."

His laugh is husky, whinny. "I just don't like being here," he says.

"Me neither and I'm getting paid to be. You ready to go back now?" They start back toward Mr. Griffin's classroom. "Stop threatening people. He should've thrown you out ten times by now."

"I know."

"Anyway, I knew Griff back when he was middleweight champion of the Midwest."

"For real?"

"You want to find out?"

He laughs. "You're goofy."

"Really, he's doing more than everything he can for you."

Tevon nods.

The rest of his Monday is incident-free, but Mr. Griffin kicks him out of class each of the next two days. On Tuesday, for cussing out a classmate who didn't like the way he was leering at her. On Wednesday, for pulling his shirt off, throwing it at Mr. Griffin's desk, and shaking his flabby tummy at the other students. Each time, Danielle calms him down and escorts him back to Mr. Griffin's room.

On Thursday, Tevon doesn't come to school. Danielle

calls his uncle, who says he doesn't know where he is but will look for him.

After work on Thursday, she picks Cecelia up from daycare and goes to Erin's apartment. Marquees is in the bedroom, listening to music and drawing, his backpack still on. Wearing her nurse uniform, Erin stands in the kitchen, holding a spatula and watching hamburgers sizzle.

"You going to see him with me?" Danielle asks, untucking her polo from her jeans.

"Not today. Marquees and I are going to a movie. You can tell him that, too."

"Erin."

"Okay, don't tell him that. But I'll give him another week to think about what he did."

"He says he did nothing."

"Shouldn't have been out there. Anyway, my baby won't be going to jail to see his brother. Hug him for me. And tell him to call me tonight. Movie should be out by nine."

"I'm going to peek into your closet."

Erin looks up from the spatula, grins at Danielle.

"What?" Danielle asks.

"Always messing with people."

"They said one of us had to be there with him, anyway, since Connor's not family."

"Sure. What's he want with EJ, anyway?"

"Just started law school."

"That just means he's not a lawyer yet. Probably extra credit. If he wants to see the inside of a cell, tell him to get there the old-fashioned way."

"He loved those boys," Danielle says.

"Then he left."

"Yeah?"

"Just don't take my new sweater. Theater's too damn cold."

"Thanks."

"Always messing."

"You're not?"

"*I* keep it simple. *You* don't know what to do with simple."

Danielle scoffs.

She stands before the open bedroom closet for two minutes, biting her pointer finger and staring absently at a pink tulle skirt, before trying on three outfits. Eventually, she puts her jeans back on, along with a touch of mascara and Erin's hoop earrings and sleeveless ivory blouse.

At dinner, Erin looks her over. "Going to jail to pick somebody up."

"Stop that. He needs friends."

"So do you."

"I think you're pretty," Marquees says, ketchup in the corner of his mouth.

"Thanks, baby."

"Tell your boyfriend I said hi," Erin says.

Danielle rolls her eyes.

At the detention center, Danielle passes through security, a metal detector and pat-down, then a guard leads her and Cecelia to an open table in the visiting area, calls for an escort for EJ, and looks her over. She ignores him, rocking Cecelia's car seat with her foot. The visiting area has thin gray carpet, bare white walls, and eight tables, with sixteen chairs facing a receptionist's office. Two stocky uniformed guards stand at the back of the room, radios and handcuffs on their belts. The stuffy air smells of teenage body odor and hints of cheap chemical cleaner. Boys in identical tan slacks and shirts play checkers, chess, or cards with relatives.

EJ enters the room with his head down. A guard walks behind him, eyeing him. He looks emaciated to her, taller and older and meaner than he was just a week ago. He sits, begins twisting the short, coiled dreads at the back of his head with his skinny fingers. Danielle stares at him and he stares at Cecelia. His shoulders are tense. His sienna eyes are bright, alert, and spiteful.

"You don't seem too sad to be here," she says.

"Being sad won't help me get out."

"Depends on what type of sad you are."

"You here to talk at me?

"That's for your mom to do."

"She said she's not coming."

"She's mad."

"I didn't do anything."

"Okay."

"You don't believe me."

"Everyone who's ever been in your position says he didn't do anything. And they're not all telling the truth."

"But I really didn't—"

"Stop saying that."

"You said you wouldn't talk at me, Auntie."

"I'm just being honest. If you don't want to deal with it..." She trails off, shaking her head and rubbing her drowsy eyes.

He looks around the room, nods at someone from his living unit.

"Just don't go around thinking everyone else cares about whether you did it. If the system says it was three boys who stabbed that other kid, they'll find three boys to pay up for it. If you're one of them, so be it."

"That's not fair."

"And what, I was born yesterday? Nothing's fair."

They're quiet. He twists his stubby bangs.

"Sorry, you're right," she says, "I said I wouldn't talk at you. I won't say anything more."

"I don't want to stay till trial. My lawyer says I can be home tomorrow if I just say I did it. Then I can make it up to mom for all her worrying."

"You'll have a record."

"No, when I'm eighteen, they'll take it all away."

"What do you think happens in the meantime?"

"You said you wouldn't talk at me."

"I guess I lied."

"Whatever. It's not so bad here."

"You like it?"

"I didn't say that."

"Making friends with the little hustlers and loudmouths and career criminals?"

"Doing what I have to."

Coming directly from class, Connor arrives in black dress pants and a white collared shirt beneath a sapphire V-neck sweater. He shakes EJ's hand, grabs an extra chair from a nearby table, and sits facing them. EJ looks at the guard, expecting him to ask Connor to move to the side of the table facing the receptionist, but the guard merely glares back at him.

"You remember me?" Connor asks cheerily.

"Yeah."

"How's your little brother?"

"Good."

"And your mom?"

EJ nods, looking at his hands flat on the table.

"You want to play cards?" Connor asks.

"No."

"You need anything in here?"

"No."

"It's been a long time, huh."

"I guess."

"What grade are you in?"

"Sixth."

"You like school?"

EJ scowls at Danielle, then looks back down. "No."

"Is it hot in here?" Connor takes off his sweater, balls it

up in his lap. "If you're wondering, I've been in Minnesota the last few years. Three, is it? Time moves fast. I'm back in town for law school."

EJ looks up suddenly. "Are you my lawyer, too?"

"No."

"Are you his lawyer, the boy that got hurt?"

"No."

"Can you help me? Can you tell them I didn't do anything?"

"They don't care what I think."

He drops his head again. "You look fatter than before."

Connor smiles. "I am."

EJ smirks at him. Danielle looks back and forth between them.

"I'm sorry, EJ. It feels awful when you really want to help somebody, but you can't."

"That's how I feel about my mom right now."

"You understand, then."

EJ folds his hands together and places them on his lap. A woman at the table behind Connor shouts, and one of the guards steps forward to tell her to quiet down. Connor glances back at them, and when he turns to face EJ again, the boy says, "She's mad at Jamal because he got in a fight in the gym."

"About what?" Danielle asks.

"Hard to explain."

"Kids trying to fight you?"

"No."

"You scared?"

"No."

"I would be," Connor says.

"You're soft."

"Probably."

"Most the time, I'm in my room. Or at school."

"What do you learn in school?"

"Nothing. Kids fight there, too."

"Not you, though?" Danielle pries.

"I have protection."

"Oh?"

"That's how it works here."

"I know how it works," Danielle replies.

EJ sets an elbow on the table, turns his head, and begins twirling his bangs again. Connor watches him. Danielle picks up Cecelia, bounces her on her knee.

Connor says, "EJ, I know I've been gone and you probably don't know me from one of these guards. It's just that I remember us being good friends back in the day. And, shit, that's the last I remember being happy. I thought I'd come visit you, while you're in here and bored, anyway. I won't come back to bug you if you don't want me to."

EJ sticks his bottom lip out, shrugs with indifference.

"Excited, huh? Can I come see you again next week?"

"Okay."

"Want me to bring anything?"

"The keys to my cell."

Connor smiles.

"Five minutes!" the guard yells.

"Seems like I've been away longer than I have. You're so much older."

EJ is quiet, then he suddenly squints and asks, "You think coming here will make you happier?"

"I don't know, EJ. When I finish law school, I'm not going to work for a corporation or big business. I want to be able to help people in need."

"You think you're at the zoo."

"EJ," Danielle intercedes.

He ignores her. Tossing his head back in the direction of the guards, he snarls, "Maybe they'll give you a tour, show you all the freaks in my pod. The boy in the cell next to me pisses under his door every other day. Another one brags to me about raping his sister. The way to get by here is to threaten to beat everyone else's ass more than they threaten to beat yours. To make sure your crew is bigger than theirs. Now, that's all I think about. It's a game I play in my cell when I'm alone, all the fantasizing and scheming."

"One minute!" the guard says, radioing for assistance "transporting the subjects" back to their cells.

EJ and Connor stare at each other, expressionlessly, and Danielle decides against mediating.

Soon, two guards escort EJ and the other boys away, and another guard escorts Danielle and Connor out of the building. They walk side by side to the unlit parking lot. When she stops at her car, he continues without looking back at her, as if she weren't there. His head down, grimacing, he appears deep in thought. She doesn't call out to say goodbye.

Before school the next morning, she attends her weekly paraprofessional meeting in the teachers' lounge. Principal Lewis, a snippy little woman in a black pencil skirt and blazer, asks Danielle and Mr. Griffin about Tevon's behavior in the first weeks of school.

"Up and down," Danielle says.

Ms. Lewis looks down at Tevon's file. "You documented that he was asked to leave the classroom multiple times at Mr. Griffin's request. Is that true, Mr. Griffin?"

"Yes," he replies.

"Knowing how patient you are, I'm sure he had done plenty to warrant calling the paras."

"He needed to get a book from his locker and Danielle was going the same way."

"Three days in a row?"

He looks at Danielle. "Each day, he behaved well once he returned."

"Other students said he threatened you."

"Never felt threatened."

"That's hardly the point."

"Most times, he just talks to talk, Ms. Lewis."

"Why aren't those threats in any of your reports?" she asks Danielle.

"I never heard them. I don't go off what other kids tell me happened."

Ms. Lewis studies Danielle's stoic face for a moment, then looks back down at the file. "Truant yesterday. Already truant three days in the first two weeks. I don't know how many more chances we can give him. Same story as last year."

Danielle explains, "He wasn't on his medication over the summer. He kept missing his appointments, so he wasn't getting his prescription filled."

"How do you know this?" Ms. Lewis asks.

"From Darrell."

"His uncle," Mr. Griffin explains.

"You know him?" Ms. Lewis asks her.

"He called me. We go back."

She closes the file. "It's not fair to the other kids in the class."

"Of course not," Danielle replies. Mr. Griffin nods.

"Let's revisit it next week."

After the meeting, Mr. Griffin and Danielle walk to his classroom.

"You know what *revisit* means. I can't keep covering for him," he says.

"Yes, you can."

"Come on, you know how this ends. It's just like Malik and Stu from last year. And Kenny and Stacey and—"

"I know," she says, cutting him off.

He glances down at her, pauses. "Okay, let's see how next week is. It'll go how it goes."

"If we can get him to his doctor, maybe. Or a counselor."

"I wouldn't get my hopes up about him. That's all I'm saying."

"I don't have hopes," she replies, "just work to do."

"Must be why you're the only person here not looking for another job."

Tevon doesn't show up for school that day, which Danielle spends bustling from class to class, dealing with teens whom the hot, sunny Friday encourages to act out. They run down the halls, jump out of their desks, shout, and roughhouse. She employs her every trick to keep them in line. Death stares and nicknames and inside jokes, sticks and carrots.

Between weekend errands, she tries reaching Tevon's uncle, Darrell, who doesn't answer.

On Sunday afternoon, while she's burping Cecelia, Charles calls.

"You into that guy?" he says without a hello. "I heard he's into you."

"What about it?"

"Nothing. Is he?"

"No," she replies.

"Are you?"

"I don't know, Charles."

"You act like I've never been good enough for you."

"We're doing this again, huh?"

"It's the truth."

"You think you have been?"

"Since Cecelia, it's like you don't even call anymore."

She says nothing.

"I'd be fucked up and you'd come for me. I'd be clean and you wouldn't. I think you liked it best when I treated you bad."

"It was never like that."

"How was it?"

"I wanted you to be special. How's that?" The line is silent. "Don't pretend you called looking for the truth," she says.

"I wasn't so bad."

"No, you weren't."

"Nobody could make you happy."

"Maybe not, Charles."

"Now that Cecelia's here, you don't call at all."

She sighs.

"How's my baby?" he asks.

"Tired."

"What if I just left? Detroit. Never came back."

"You do what you want, Charles. That's your thing."

"Brad has a job for me."

"I can help you pack."

He hangs up.

Darrell calls that night to tell her Tevon will be in school on Monday morning. "No question."

"Great news. Thank you."

"He was out with his other uncles, you know. I told them to stay clear of him. They just use him to run errands for them, you know. 'Go sell these stereos we stole. Go buy us some smokes.' Whatever else. They'll get him in real trouble once they trust him enough with some bigger scams. Crooked fuckers."

Tevon returns to school and Danielle is pleased to document his studious and respectful behavior on Monday and Tuesday.

On Tuesday evening, she and Erin visit EJ, while Marquees and Cecelia stay back with one of Erin's friends.

Erin and EJ weep. He buries his face in his shirt. "I'm scared of what's going to happen, Mom. And where they'll send me if they find me guilty. I want to go home."

Erin hugs him tightly for fifteen minutes, then a fight between two kids from EJ's living unit cuts visiting hours short. Danielle, EJ, and Erin watch as the guards swarm into the room, slam the thrashing boys on the carpet, and apply wrist lock pressure until they stop writhing. Their faces smashed against the floor, the boys shout threats at each other, spit flying from their mouths, until the guards jerk them up on their feet and rush them out of the room. Two guards stay back to usher the visitors out of the building.

On Wednesday, a pregnant classmate of Tevon's steals one of his chicken nuggets. He shoves her onto the cafeteria floor, and a brawl breaks out, after which, bleeding from his nose and covered in sloppy joe ground beef, he climbs atop a table to fling lunch trays at the kids around him, like Frisbees. While Danielle, Mr. Griffin, and the school officer take turns attempting to talk him down, Ms. Lewis calls the police. When she warns him that they'll arrive any minute, his eyes widen, his jaw drops. He jumps down, bolts out of the cafeteria and into the street.

That night, after dinner, Danielle and Cecelia curl up on the couch and watch TV. She calls Darrell again but he doesn't answer. She stares at the ceiling, kissing Cecelia's head until the girl falls asleep.

The next evening, she drops Cecelia off at Erin's, and she, Connor, and EJ sit at the table closest to the receptionist: today a hulking, buzz-cut ogre who appears half-asleep. She and EJ again face the office, and Connor again faces the guards in the back. Having skipped class, Connor wears jeans and a plain blue shirt. He sits up straight, leans over the table, his hands folded. He narrows his eyes at EJ.

"Didn't think you'd come back," EJ says, twisting his bangs with both hands, his elbows on the table.

"How come?"

"Thought you'd run back to Minnesota."

"What did they charge you with?"

"A bunch of stuff I didn't do. Rioting and looting and assault with a weapon, all this and that. I'm telling you, I just stood there. I didn't know anything was going to happen, and I didn't know it was happening, and I didn't want anything bad to happen to anyone, really. I didn't do what they say I did. Any of it. Nobody believes me."

"Yeah?"

"Do you?"

"What does it matter if I believe you?"

EJ shakes his head. "You're going to be like one of those guys."

"Which guys?"

"Guys who want to keep me in here."

"One minute, you're calling me out for leaving. The next, you want me to tell you you're innocent. Doesn't make any sense. How old are you?"

"Almost thirteen."

"You think I'd be doing you any favors treating you like you're thirteen?"

"Whatever. You can't help me. You think I'm guilty."

Danielle says, "The more you ask people to tell you you're innocent, the guiltier you look."

"You're talking at me like my mom does, Auntie, like all everyone tries to."

"Fine. Tell me how it is, then."

"I tried."

"Tell me more."

"This is dumb."

"Dumber than being in your cell?"

"Cell's not so bad."

"So, you thought that after last week I wouldn't want to come back to see you?" Connor asks. "You thought you'd scare me off, make me think, 'EJ doesn't give a shit about me, so why should I give a shit about him? Connor's just a pampered little bitch who doesn't know anything?'"

EJ nods.

"Let's hear it, then," Connor says.

"What?"

"You're mad that no one's listening to you, so I tell you I want to hear you, and what do you do? You try to run me off; you clam up. Yeah, I've been gone some years. So what? I'm here now. We might not be friends—"

"We're not."

"But we're not strangers."

"You're trying to make it like we're cool again."

"Why can't we be?"

"That's dumb," EJ jeers.

"How come?"

He stops twirling his bangs, crosses his arms. Danielle glances at Connor, who's still leaning across the table toward EJ.

Connor says, "I met your teacher in the lobby. She said you're learning about the Civil Rights Movement and Martin Luther King. She said you have things to say in class."

"Maybe, I don't know."

"She said you don't like King as much as the other kids do."

"He's okay."

"But not what everyone makes him out to be."

EJ rubs his thighs. Danielle watches Connor, who waits for EJ to collect his thoughts.

"Mrs. Smith shows us all these pictures of guys in nice suits with dogs running after them and night sticks and hoses. All the lynching and beatings. Why did they do that? Take all that lying down?"

"I don't know."

"They were soft."

"But that's not what your teacher says?"

"No, but she's wrong. Peace isn't the only way."

"No, it's not," Connor echoes the boy. "I guess they just did what they thought was best."

"That's fucking stupid."

"Some people agree with you."

"You don't," EJ says.

"I don't know what's best all the time."

"You fought to get your bike back, remember?"

"You remember the bike, huh!" Connor exclaims. Danielle looks at the receptionist, who doesn't react to Connor's outburst. "But I didn't fight to get it back."

"That's what you said."

"I must've been joking, or lied. I just hung onto it and didn't let go."

"You got beat up."

"Yeah, but I got the bike back."

"You could've afforded a new one."

"And what if someone took that one, too? I'd run out of bikes. Plus, I loved that bike."

"They took my dad away over almost nothing. Just doing what he had to do for us. They swept through the neighborhood and took whatever they could. The cops. *Your* people. People just like the guards here. Took him away. Wasn't any holding on to him going to save him, either. My mom tried that."

Danielle watches Connor sit back, slide his hands under the table, and frown at EJ.

EJ calmly continues, "It's not even about us being friends, you and me. It's all about you feeling better about yourself. I've seen this before from people at school, teachers and volunteers and all that. I saw the way you dressed before and the way you talk and the way you look at the other kids here. You come from a lot of nice shit. No cop ever follows you around asking you where you're going to and what's your name. No cop puts his hands on you for no reason. You got everything comfortable and you're like everyone else who will do what he can to keep it that way. Now you just get to slip back into Chicago and act like you never left. Like we're friends. Look at the guards. They don't mind you sitting on that side of the table, even though we're all supposed to be on this side. If you started yelling like that lady did last week, they wouldn't walk over here and tell you to be quiet like they did to her. You could stand up and go over and talk to them…Danielle, they'd slam on the ground and take to jail."

"You might be right—"

"I know I am. I've seen it. And you don't really want anything to change, either. Not really, because most of the time you have no idea how much different my life is from yours. You don't notice things like we have to. You and I don't live in the same world. We never will. At least, not till enough of us, in places like this and in our streets, fight back and take what we should. If King was right to do things the way he did, what are we all doing in here?"

EJ stops. He leans the elbows of his crossed arms against the table.

"Go on," Connor implores him.

"That's all I have to say."

"You know you're special, right?"

"I know I didn't do what they said I did. I've done stupid stuff before, some stuff that could've got me in here, maybe. Danielle knows the truth. But I didn't touch that kid. I'm innocent."

"But you like this, don't you? Arguing? Debating?"

EJ shrugs.

"*You* should be in law school, not me."

He pulls his dreads down against his forehead and looks up to see how far they reach.

"What do you want?" Connor asks.

"To get out."

"I mean, overall."

"To *be* out."

"Who's stopping you from getting what you want?"

"You. People like you. People who are comfortable with the way things are."

"Who's going to help you?"

"Me. People like me. Those who *aren't* comfortable."

"You're all on the same side here?" Connor asks.

"We should be."

"But you're not."

"We could be."

"That's what you're working on?"

"I'm working on survival. One day at a time. I know you're trying to box me in. You think I'm a hypocrite. If you were here, you'd understand."

"I didn't say you were a hypocrite."

"I can tell by the way you're looking at me."

"I'm looking at you like you're a lot smarter than I was when I was your age, because you've had to think over things I've never had to."

"I don't know what you're trying to do with these compliments."

"You're just like your aunt. Don't trust anybody but yourself."

"EJ," Danielle says. "Those boys here don't have a damn clue what you're talking about with this social change stuff."

"They have a sense."

"They know about putting their hands up and getting younger kids like you to do their dirty work for them."

"I can put my hands up, too, and I'm nobody's punk. I see you're finally coming to your boyfriend's defense."

She rolls her eyes and taps her nails on the table.

"Three minutes," a guard bellows.

"Here's what I don't understand, EJ," Connor says. "If people like me can't help you, and your guys don't understand you, who are your allies? Or, are you just going to do everything yourself?"

"Maybe I will."

Danielle says, "You don't get caught up in a riot because you're doing things on your own."

"Like I said, I didn't do that."

"You were there, weren't you? They didn't arrest you at your house. You were running away with the rest of those fools. And you weren't there planning some revolution, were you?"

"Not—"

"What was all the fighting about?"

"I don't even know."

"It couldn't have been that important to you, then."

"One minute," the guard says.

"Whatever," EJ finally replies. "I'm not perfect. Neither are you two."

Connor says, "That's true, EJ. I'm a fuck up. I spent my years away making money, drinking, and gambling. Trying to be married to a woman who didn't love me. Trying to be a father to the baby I lost. I'm definitely not perfect. But I'd like to be better."

EJ looks up at him, twisting his dreads.

"Can I come see you again?" Connor asks.

He shrugs. "Sorry about your baby."

"Me, too."

Afterward, Danielle and Connor walk to their cars. He stares at his feet, hands in his pockets.

"How are classes?" she asks.

"Bunch of yuppies who've read more books than I have."

"You'll catch up."

"They don't know anything. Not that I do."

"I'm hungry. You want to get something to eat?"

"Not tonight."

"Another time?"

"That kid's got a lot going on in his head. He reminds me of you so much."

"I worry about him."

"So do I."

As they reach his car, he pulls out his keys and she says, "I can tell you're hurting."

He opens the door, climbs into his car. "You're drawn to people who hurt. As long as I've known you."

"I'm drawn to the good in others."

"Maybe that's it."

"Name any block in Chicago, and I'll tell you where the nearest decent food is. There are things I'd like to tell you."

"Sometime, maybe," he replies. "It's dark out. Want me to drive you to your car?"

Walking away, she scoffs.

He shuts the door and drives off.

That night Cecelia won't fall asleep, so Danielle straps her into her car seat and goes for a drive. As Cecelia blabbers in the backseat, Danielle calls the homeless shelters programmed into her phone, asks if anyone's seen Tevon. After exhausting her list, she drops her phone in the center console and parks on a wide street with apartment complexes on either side, car still running, lights off. A solar system of streetlight orbs descends into the horizon, and the flames of a full moon engulf the sky. A pack of screeching teens crosses the street. For a few minutes, Cecelia's gurgling soothes Danielle. But, as the teens disappear down a side street, as her daughter hushes and the car goes silent, she begins to glower at the lights and the moon. She squeezes her eyes shut and bites her cheek, groaning as if in pain, as if possessed by the darkness of her eyelids. Then she drives again. Past Nigerian immigrants smoking cigarettes beneath corner store awnings, schoolyard jungle gym domes shimmering in the moonlight, officers in SUVs patrolling neighborhoods. A man in a sleeveless undershirt, inspecting the engine of the car parked in his garage, peers over his shoulder as she drives by. She checks the rearview mirror again. Cecelia is asleep.

In the morning Danielle has a message from Darrell. Tevon, who had been stealing and selling TVs for his uncles, stayed with him last night.

"He's already gone," Darrell says, when Danielle calls him back on her way to work. "Right after breakfast."

"Any idea where he went?"

"He said he's not going back to my brothers, but I hope he does. Maybe he'll get arrested. He'd be safer locked up."

"If you see him, tell him to call me. He's been expelled."

She emails a picture of Tevon to every homeless shelter she knows. They promise to call her back if they see him.

On Tuesday, she, Erin, and Cecelia visit EJ. He lost five pounds in a week. He says he has the flu and can't keep food down. His face is ashen, indigo-tinctured. He can barely keep his head up.

"Another ten days," Erin tells him, taking his frail, listless hand. "Can you hold on till then?"

The following night, while awaiting a call from Darrell or one of the shelters, Danielle gets a call from EJ, who says he's in the detention center's special housing unit.

"Because of the flu?"

"No, Auntie."

"What happened?"

He sniffles.

"EJ."

"I can't talk long."

"How much time do you have?"

"Ten minutes is all."

"What happened, EJ?"

"I'm really worried about court now. I don't want them to send me away or give me time somewhere. I didn't do anything."

"You got in trouble?"

"Sort of. They're keeping me here to protect me."

"From what?"

"Don't tell Mom I'm in SHU."

"How long have you been there?"

"Since last night. The cell's tiny. There's nothing in there. Just a toilet and sink. No mattress or pillows."

"But you're safe?"

"It's cold. They gave me a sweatshirt."

"Are you safe, EJ?"

"Yeah," he replies as he begins to sob. When he stops a minute later, he says, "The boy in the cell next to me keeps smashing his head against the door. I saw the guards tie him to this big chair so he wouldn't, but he's doing it again now."

"Just nine days to go."

"But they might sentence me somewhere now."

"Why? What happened EJ?"

Danielle can hear the guard say, "Five minutes."

"I can't help you if I don't know what's going on," she says.

"I was talking with someone in class. I laughed at something he said to Mrs. Smith. The guys didn't like that since I shouldn't be talking to him and his people. They talked to me about it. They wanted me to fight him in the gym." The line is silent. Then EJ continues, "I told my guys I wouldn't do it for no reason. They said I was scared and all this. They said they'd beat me if I didn't. I didn't know what to do."

"Okay."

"Then they just, like, jumped us both. This kid, Felix, and me. The guards put us in these cells after we got beat, Felix worse than me. They put him in the cell next to me. Now he's hitting his head. I can't deal with all this, Auntie."

"EJ, baby."

"I didn't want to fight him. I wasn't scared or anything. I wasn't scared, Auntie, but I didn't want to fight him. What for? And I didn't want to fight my friends, either, and I didn't want them to fight me. All because I laughed at this joke of his? Now my friends say they'll kill me and I fucked everything up. They punched me and kicked me till the guards pulled me away. I shouldn't have laughed, I guess. I shouldn't have been talking to him, and I knew better, too. Now, I'm in the SHU, and the guards are writing up reports on me since I got in a fight, and the judge might send me somewhere all because I shouldn't have been laughing in school. And everyone's mad at me. They said they'll kill me when I get out…"

The guard tells EJ to wrap up his call.

"EJ," she says. "Everything you just said. You didn't do anything that a normal and decent and…what a good kid wouldn't do. You're in a bad position and it might get worse, but you didn't do anything wrong in the gym."

"I don't feel that way. They're going to make me pay for it, too."

"Your guys?"

"Yeah."

"In the morning, ask for a pencil and paper. Write the judge a letter, tell her what happened. She'll read it next to the reports. Okay?"

"Okay."

"I love you. Call your mom tomorrow. Tell her what you told me."

"Okay."

"Okay?"

"What will they do to me?" he asks.

"Who?"

"My guys."

"You're so young, EJ. If you're smart now, they already did their worst."

"You think so?"

"No question."

"Okay."

"Anyway, your *friends* aren't the only people who know people. Go to bed. And thank the guard for the phone call."

"Okay."

"Love you."

"Love you, too, Auntie."

On the morning of EJ's appearance before the judge, Connor and Danielle meet at a bustling coffee shop near the courthouse. Connor wears a sport coat, salmon tie, and charcoal slacks. Danielle, a black skirt and pear blouse. In a flower dress, Cecelia stands on the bright red booth cushion, gripping her mother's forearm for balance.

"I feel bad that I couldn't see him where he was staying. He didn't get hurt too badly?"

"Some scrapes. Staff got to him quickly."

"What does his lawyer say?"

"He'll be fine. Probably a little probation. Erin's sweating it, though. EJ, too."

"You don't seem too worried."

"I am, but sparrows get theirs. It's nice of you to come for him and Erin. I think, in time, you and EJ could be good friends again."

"Wonder why he didn't just fight that kid like they told him to."

"He doesn't like anyone telling him what to do. Even his buddies."

"That's good, isn't it?"

"I suppose so. By the way, he won't thank you for coming to see him, no matter how much he appreciated it."

"I know the type." He tries to sip his coffee, but it's too hot. "What did you want to talk about?"

"You could've gone to school anywhere."

He cocks his head to the side, recoils slightly. Nervous, he keeps blowing on his coffee. "I said I wasn't interested in this. Still never been told no, huh?"

"Just don't listen to it."

"You can't go around taking whatever you want from people."

"You can if they give it to you."

He loosens his tie. "What's Charles up to these days?"

"I want to see you again after today."

"I don't think that's a good idea."

"Yes, you do."

"Can't see how it works," he replies.

She laughs, joyous chittering weakened by work and lack of sound sleep.

He looks away from her. "Laugh it up."

Cecelia falls on her butt and Danielle stands her up. "You like her dress?"

He smiles. "Of course I do."

She holds Cecelia's slobbery hands as the girl stands wobbling. She drops her face close to her daughter's and says, "I expect you to keep telling me you don't want anything to do with me. You'll stick to your school work and carry on with your life. But before long you'll call me or I'll call you. Maybe EJ will need your help. Maybe before you're even done with school. And maybe you'll come stay with me at Gloria's house a couple weekends a month. On Saturday mornings, you can study at the library, and in the afternoon we can get lunch and take Cecelia to the park, and in the evening we can put her down to sleep and talk and know that we'll still have Sunday together. All of that. Either way, I'll be waiting." With a paper napkin, she wipes drool from Cecelia's chin. "Now, see, while you're out there living your life, you can't pretend you don't know what I'm up to."

She smiles at Cecelia's blubbering, picks her up, and places her on her knee.

"But I'm not asking for everything right now," she says. "I just want to see you again."

"It seems you want much more than that. You're right about the first part, that I'll tell you no."

"We'll see about the rest."

"You're selfish."

"Yes," she replies, "but I'm a lot of other, better things, too. And you know it."

After playing peek-a-boo with Cecelia for a bit, he asks, "Why did you change your mind?"

"About what?"

"About *me*."

"What I think about you hasn't changed in a long time."

"Okay. About *us*, then."

"You think I'm wrong to want you in my life?"

He sips his coffee, doesn't answer.

"You think I shouldn't feel the way I have, the way I do?" she continues.

"I guess not."

"Then, what's the difference?"

They meet Marquees and Erin at the courthouse. Connor waits outside during sentencing, a swift and unceremonious event. The judge finds EJ not guilty on all charges but one, rioting. She gives him six months of probation that, if completed without violation, would expunge his record entirely.

EJ changes into the clothes in which he was arrested, sneakers and jeans and a hoodie, and leaves the detention center arm in arm with his mother.

They meet Connor on the courthouse steps. He shakes Marquees' hand and talks with Erin. "I have some contacts in Cook County, not a ton, but a few. Whatever I can do to help, in the future."

She smiles politely. "We'll be fine. Thank you."

"This man here!" EJ shouts, jumping up and down, pointing at Connor. "Coming in and acting like he knows something!"

"EJ," Erin says, "I'm going to take you to your probation officer's office right now. You need to see where it is in case I can't drive you there at some point."

"I'm free!"

"EJ, listen."

"Coming in and acting like he knows. I told you I didn't do it!"

"EJ."

He stops jumping but keeps his fingers pointed at Connor.

Connor smiles at him, starts walking away, his eyes moistening. "I'm glad I got to see you all again. Have a nice day."

"There he goes. He's scared of me!"

"EJ," Erin implores him, nodding in Connor's direction.

Connor only makes it a few steps before EJ catches up to him, taps him on the shoulder, and says, "So, she wanted me to tell you that you really do look fatter than before."

Connor laughs.

"No," EJ says. "Well, you know. Even though you don't know shit and you dress like a stiff and all that, you're not a total dick."

"Thanks."

"Will you be my lawyer when I get older?"

"EJ!" Danielle scolds him.

"Just kidding. I got to go."

"See you around," Connor replies. He waves goodbye to them.

Erin gives EJ two choices: being grounded until Christmas or trying out for the school's basketball team. Danielle introduces herself to his basketball coach, who, interested in her, volunteers to stay after practice and help EJ with his jumper.

The nights turn cold and Tevon shows up at his uncle's. Darrell agrees to take him in. At first, Danielle hardly recognizes the reedy child; time with his uncles has made him moodier, cruder. She sets him up with a counselor she trusts and contacts the paraprofessionals at his new school to ensure they understand his need for special classes and medication.

When Cecelia starts walking, Danielle baby-proofs the house. The busy little girl tips over cups of water and throws markers and scrambles oversized puzzle pieces and splashes bathwater in her mother's eyes. She and Danielle go for walks around the block, to playdates with Danielle's coworkers and to Erin's. One, a handsome single father, asks Erin for Danielle's number.

"Just one date?" Erin asks over the phone.

"No."

"What's your plan, then? It's not going to get any easier to meet somebody."

"Bye, sis."

For months, wintry gusts crash against her bedroom window. In the morning, ice glosses her windshield. She starts her car, sprinkles salt on the sidewalk. She takes Cecelia to daycare, then attacks her tireless duties in and outside of school, rushing headlong from one tragedy to the next. In bed, she lies awake, outwitting tomorrow's evils, the conspiracies of iniquity: airport layoffs, foster care abuses, homelessness, lotto ticket splurges, healthcare price gouging, bottles and pills, administrator salaries, boys' battered cheekbones, girls' arms in slings. When she thinks of Connor, every week or so, it's only while considering EJ's coach's invitation to dinner or Mr. Griffin's subtle flirting.

One night in spring, Darrell calls to tell her he kicked Tevon out.

"I gave him so many chances. But he brought his junk into my house. I can't have that around. I can't lose my job, Danielle."

"I understand. What was he wearing when he left?"

"I gave him my jacket. Dark green, with a hood."

She calls the shelters, then dresses Cecelia in a tiny parka and snow pants, puts her in her car seat, and drives around looking for him. The following night, just after work, she gets a text from Connor: *have some days off, can i see you?*

of course but i have something i need to do

She drops Cecelia off at Erin's, fills her gas tank, and waits for him at her house. He arrives just after dinner in his winter jacket and stocking cap.

"What's he look like?" he asks, climbing into her car.

"Tall, thin. He might be wearing a green jacket with a hood."

They drive for several blocks before he says, "I met someone."

"What's she like?"

"Not much like you."

"Not cute? Not friendly or charming? Not funny?"

He smiles. "You probably already knew."

"Haven't talked to Charlotte in a while, if that's what you meant. So, you came to tell me you met someone?"

"I guess. Not just that."

The car warms up. He unzips his coat and begins talking

about the other students in his program, most of whom are wealthier, sharper, and better educated. "The thing is, though," he explains, "many of them are incredibly naïve. It's not their first instinct, for instance, to question how the police might use a law to harass the poor. Or how a corporation might use a law to cheat its employees or its investors or the government. Frankly, it's mind-numbing to watch. They side with the powerful. They're always forgetting that the powerful make the laws in the first place."

As impassioned as she can ever recall him, he brings up some cases to illustrate his point, talking with his hands, balling his fists and rapping his knuckles on the glove compartment.

"What about your girlfriend? Is she naïve, too?"

He grins. "I'm afraid to ask her too much. I don't want to argue with her."

"Yes, you do."

After an hour she says, "I should get back to Erin's soon. That's enough for tonight. It was worth a shot."

"I hope he's okay."

"You should pray for him."

"You know I don't bother with prayer."

"But you have no problem with hope?"

He smiles, says nothing. She laughs at him.

On the way back to her house, she suddenly asks, "Want to see something?"

"Sure."

"I'm going to find a way to open it again."

"Open *what?*"

"I'll show you."

She parks across the street from the rec center and they look the abandoned building over. Chains strangle the front doors. As he steps out of the car, he shakes his head.

"They forgot to change one of the locks," she whispers.

"Really?"

She leads him around the center to the gym's side entrance, looks around to see that nobody's watching them, and pulls a key from her pocket. "Come on," she says.

They slip inside. The gym is dank and frigid and dark. She turns on her cellphone flashlight and they wander around, skirting a patch of mold. He picks up a flat basketball, and when he tries to dribble it, it thuds on the plastic tiling, inert. When her phone rings, the flashlight turns off and the gym darkens.

"That's great news. Thank you so much," she says. She hangs up and turns the flashlight on again. "That was a woman from one of the shelters. She said Tevon will be staying there tonight."

"Good to hear."

"I haven't been here in over a year."

"No?"

"Who would I go with?"

"I suppose. By the way, how's EJ?"

"His coach told him he's got an academic scholarship jump shot."

"What's that?"

"It means he better hit the books in high school."

He laughs. "I love those boys."

"I know you do."

She leads him out the side door, locking it behind her, and they walk around the building to the front entrance. She sits on the steps, hugging herself to ward off the cold, watching him cup his eyes as he peers in through the glass front door. Then he pulls his hat down over the bottoms of his ears, crosses his arms, and sits next to her.

"How will you get them to open it again?"

"I don't know yet."

He lays his head on her shoulder. His coat smells of

spring, of exhaust and gravel and playground soil. He says, "I'm beginning to notice more and more how cruel people are to one another. The more I notice, the crueler I realize I've been."

"What did you do that was so terrible?"

"Not enough."

She kisses his forehead, tastes his dried sweat. "We have the rest of our lives to be cruel to each other."

ACKNOWLEDGMENTS

I would like to thank my wife and best friend, Ashley Ver Burg, for her years of encouragement and inspiration. I'd also like thank Regal House editor-in-chief, Jaynie Royal, for her avid advocacy; Regal House senior editor Pam Van Dyk for her insightful and diligent editorial assistance; my good friends and readers Kyle Ellingson, Aaron Sinner, and Robin Soukup, who've always taken the time to provide feedback on my manuscripts; my St. John's University mentors Rene McGraw and Scott Richardson, who've always taken the time to impart their wisdom to me; and the staff and residents of the Ramsey County Juvenile Detention Center, where I learned much about the privileges of being a white man in America.